THE SINGING TREES MYSTERY

THE TED WILFORD SERIES

THE SINGING
TREES MYSTERY

TED WILFORD MYSTERY SERIES

 ## NORVIN PALLAS

WILDSIDE PRESS

ACKNOWLEDGMENTS

The Wildside Press reprints of the Ted Wilford series were made possible by the assistance of many people, including Norvin Pallas's family; Steve Romberger, whose copy of *The Secret of Thunder Mountain* was ultimately used to create this edition; George Beatty and James D. Keeline, who provided copies of many of the texts and covers; and David M. Baumann, whose essay "A Dark Horse Series" was an invaluable reference for reprinting the stories; and of course Wildside's production team, Shawn Garrett, Helen McGee, Sam Hogan, and Steve Coupe.

To RAE

Published by Wildside Press LLC.
www.wildsidepress.com

CHAPTER 1

The Kid Wagon

Half an hour earlier, the office of the Forestdale High School *Statesman* had been swarming with hurrying reporters, moving about among the half-dozen speeding typists, as everyone tried to beat the late Friday afternoon deadline and get home to start the week's spring vacation.

But now the excited voices were stilled, the telephone had ceased its seemingly endless clanging, and the typewriters were silent beneath their canvas dust covers. Editor Ted Wilford sat alone in the deserted office, still struggling over his lead editorial. He read it over once more, scratching out a word here, adding a comma there, studying it carefully.

At last, still not satisfied, but deciding that he had probably done as well as he could with it, he made up his mind to call it a night. He pushed back his chair and gathered up the approved stories to place them in a folder for delivery to the printer. He was glad this week's work was over at last, and looked forward to the next nine days—not exactly a vacation, but at least a welcome change of pace.

Ordinarily, he might have lingered a little longer, enjoying the unusual solitude of the newspaper office. But he remembered Nelson Morgan would be waiting impatiently for him on the street below, so he hurried to finish.

The door opened, and Miss Trisdale, the newspaper's faculty adviser, came into the room.

"Ted! You still at work? I thought you had left earlier with the others."

"No, Miss Trisdale, I wasn't quite satisfied with my editorial, and I felt it needed a little more work. Do you want to check it?"

"If you want me to." She smiled as she accepted the sheet of paper from him, noting his somewhat anxious air. She read his editorial carefully, then handed it back to him with a quick nod of approval. "It'll do, Ted."

"What did you really think of it?" he asked.

"Well, Ted, I don't exactly agree with everything you said. But juvenile delinquency is an important matter, and I think it's a good thing for us to know how you teenagers feel about it. Let's put it in the paper as it is." She caught his slight disappointment, and changed the subject. "What are you doing next week?"

"I'm going to be out of town," he answered.

"Oh, a vacation trip?"

"Not exactly. Nelson and I have been chosen junior counselors at the Y camp, and we're going out there to help fix up the place for the summer season. We're on our way now to pick up a small group of underprivileged boys. Mr. Krillman thought they might enjoy a little holiday, even though the camp isn't officially open."

"How nice! If you're in a hurry, Ted, I can drop the folder off at the printer's."

"Thanks, Miss Trisdale, but it's right along our way. Good night"

"Good night, Ted. Have a pleasant vacation."

"Thank you, and you, too," Ted replied.

He found Nelson leaning against the fender of Mr. Krillman's car with patient resignation.

"I hope I didn't keep you waiting too long," Ted apologized, "but it seems that everything always takes longer than you expect."

"Oh, don't worry about me. I know how tough it is to pry you out of that newspaper office. A policeman came along and was going to hang a 'slow—School Zone' sign on me, but I convinced him it was all a mistake. Say, this car is some job, isn't it?"

"Wish it were mine," Ted agreed.

They got in, and Ted maneuvered the car into a smooth pickup. "Bejeepers, I could almost steer this thing with my little finger."

"This is real limousine service," Nelson gloated, "like they have in the big cities from the airport to the classy downtown hotels."

"More like kid-wagon service," Ted corrected. He caught Nelson's questioning glance. "That's a name the country people have for the school bus that goes around to the farms picking up the pupils."

"Well, where to first?" asked Nelson, stretching his arms and leaning back luxuriously.

"Printer's office," Ted stated briefly. He drew up in front of the shop, went inside with the folder, and was back again in a few minutes. Returning to the driver's seat, he drew a list from his pocket. "Let's see. Joey Jordan and Harold Murphy live in Socono, and Philip Montague, Emmet Vance, and Ned Brown all live on farms. We may have to hunt for them a bit. I guess our best bet is to go to Socono first."

"And then, Camp Pioneer, here we come!"

On the wide-open road it would have been a temptation to gun up the engine to see what it could do, but Ted resisted, and maintained a steady, even pace. He couldn't forget that an expensive car and the care of five youngsters were greater responsibilities than anyone had ever entrusted him with before.

"I suppose it's because we're seniors," he remarked. "A year ago nobody would have thought of letting us do something like this."

"Don't kid yourself," Nelson returned. "It isn't just being seniors. It's because you're pretty famous around this part of the state, the way you found out who robbed the school's safe."

"I never found out who robbed it. That was Ken Kutler's story. All I found out was who *didn't* rob it. Anyway, these young boys don't care about anything like that. You're here because you're a big football star, and I was just invited along for the ride."

"I doubt it, but just the same it was nice we could both come along. Say, what about that editorial you were working on? How did you make out with it?"

"Oh, I don't know. I've got a copy in my coat pocket, if you want to read it."

"Do I have to?" Nelson replied, sounding bored but at the same time reaching for the inside pocket of the coat Ted had thrown across the back of the seat. He found the paper, and began reading.

"What do you think?" Ted asked of him.

"Wow! You spread it on kind of thick, didn't you?"

"Think so?" asked Ted worriedly. "That isn't what I was trying to do. It's just that teenagers get blamed for so many things that I wanted to show the other side of the picture."

"That's all very nice, pointing out the worth-while things so many teenagers are doing, but you make it sound as though all teenagers wear halos, which they've accidentally forgotten to polish up. And you can't overlook the fact that teenagers do manage to get into quite a bit of trouble—usually not quite as serious as some of the things adults do, but generally more of it. That's what I mean."

A sleek blue convertible with the top down and a boy at the wheel sped past them, exceeding the speed limit by some fifteen or twenty miles.

"Look at that, and while we're approaching a curve, too. What can you do with a driver like that? Think of the kids who soup up their engines, and hook up a spark plug to the exhaust so flames shoot out, and take the mufflers off the engines so they sound like a jet taking off. It looks as though they're trying to say, 'Look at me! I'm important.'"

"Maybe the answer to that would be to help them *feel* important," Ted suggested.

"Well, I guess that's your baby. But no fooling, Ted, I wouldn't try to tell you how to write your stuff. Maybe it is a good idea to remind people about the other side of the story. And I like that part where you criticize the word 'juvenile' in juvenile delinquency. It sounds as though these kids do these things because they're not old enough to know better, and of course that isn't true at all. A delinquent is a delinquent, no matter how old he is."

As they approached the outskirts of the town of Socono, Nelson remarked, "Anyway, I know I feel important, arriving in a fancy car like this. Mr. Krillman must be pretty well off, isn't he?"

"I don't know much about that. I suppose that without a large family of children his expenses aren't too high. Maybe it's because they haven't any children of their own that he became interested in Y affairs."

"Wasn't he a prisoner during the war?"

"Yes, the war was a tough break for him. He was wounded and taken prisoner in his first engagement, and for a time he was reported dead. It sometimes seems to me that he keeps so busy because he's trying to forget."

"You think it works?"

"It would be pretty hard to forget everything he's been through, wouldn't it? Now where's Joey's street? It should be along here somewhere."

CHAPTER 2

A Scene of Destruction

They had little trouble finding Joey's address, and the car had hardly reached the curb when a boy carrying a suitcase dashed out of the house, quickly opened the rear door, and bounced into the seat, demanding that they be on their way.

"Whoa. What's your hurry?" asked Ted.

"I want to shoot tigers in the jungle," Joey replied, matter-of-factly.

"Tigers! There aren't any tigers where we're going."

"Aren't there?" asked Joey in disappointment. "There were where I used to live."

"Where did you use to live?" asked Nelson. "In India?"

"No, in a big city. It was north of here—I think."

Nelson shook his head in perplexity. "What goes with this kid? I don't know of any jungles north of here, let alone tigers, too."

"There were," Joey assured them. "They were big tigers, with yellow stripes. Only," he felt obliged to confess, "we didn't shoot them."

"And it wasn't a jungle, was it?"

"Yes, it was, it was a real jungle," Joey insisted.

Taking Joey's suitcase from him, Ted stepped out of the car and went around the back to place it in the luggage compartment.

"Now can we go?" asked Joey eagerly.

"No, not yet. Come on out of there for a minute. We have to say good-by to your mother."

"What for?" asked Joey blankly. "She knows I'm going."

"Maybe she'll want to be sure you're on your way, and to see what kind of hoboes you've taken up with."

"Us—hoboes, in this car?" Nelson muttered, but he followed the others toward the house.

By the time they reached the door, Mrs. Jordan had put in an appearance, and she extended her hand as they introduced themselves. As soon as he could, Nelson asked:

"What's this about a tiger? Joey tells us he used to go tiger hunting in the jungle, only he didn't shoot them."

Mrs. Jordan was puzzled for a moment. Then she laughed. "Oh, there was a zoological park in the city where we lived, with the animals in natural settings. That must be what he meant. I suppose it did look a little like a jungle to him."

"So that's it," said Nelson, rather relieved. "I thought he was making it all up."

"You'll find that Joey has quite a lively imagination," his mother smiled, "a little too lively, I sometimes think."

"Well, I guess we'd better run along," Ted decided. "We have four other stops to make, and we want to get out to camp in time for supper."

"It was nice meeting you, Ted, and you, too, Nelson. I hope Joey won't give you too much trouble. Good-by, Joey," she called after her son, who was already clambering back into the car.

After picking up the four other boys, they headed toward camp. The miles flew by, and they saw they would arrive in plenty of time for supper.

"Maybe we'll have to make it ourselves," Nelson pointed out. "Mr. Krillman and Mr. Blair didn't expect to get there before six. Is there anything to eat out there?"

"Mr. Krillman carried out the staples last weekend. He's going to bring the perishables—milk, fresh vegetables, and things like that—with him tonight. I guess we can make a supper of canned beans just for tonight, if we have to. But Mr. Krillman will be there on time. He always is."

"Oh, I know, he's a reliable person. Everybody says what a good job he's doing with the Y camp. But I was just thinking maybe the boys might get hungry before he got there."

Finally they reached the point where they turned off from the main road. A winding dirt road, only wide enough for one car, led away to the camp two miles farther on.

"Hope we don't meet anybody on this road," said Nelson with a frown. "We'd have to pull off onto the shoulder, and I'd hate to get stuck in that mud."

"Who's there to meet?" asked Ted practically. "The road doesn't go anywhere except to camp, and nobody else will be there."

This proved true, and except for Mr. Metlow, whose farm lay at the beginning of the dirt road, they saw no one else at all. The camp presently came into sight, and through the trees sunlight sparkled upon the silver lake. Ted drove on up in front of the mess hall, and everyone piled out.

"Where are the windows?" Harold questioned.

"The windows?" Ted replied. "Oh, they're boarded up for the winter. Let's get the luggage out of here, Nelson, and then I believe I'll take the car right up into the shed. I don't think we'll need it again tonight, and we could have some rain before morning."

All the suitcases were piled on the ground, and then Ted drove off. As he had expected, the shed was empty, showing that Mr. Krillman hadn't arrived yet. Only as he opened the shed did Ted remember that he hadn't given Nelson the key to the mess hall, and they wouldn't be able to get in. Ted also had keys to the boathouse, the supply building, and the cabin they were to occupy. He hurried back to the mess hall, and found everyone still standing around or sitting on the luggage.

Harold ran to meet him. "Where's all the windows?" he asked again. Nelson had also come along to meet Ted, his face showing much annoyance.

"Say, Ted, there's something strange going on here. What the devil has happened to all the windows? The place looks like a thousand imps were turned loose."

"Weren't the windows all boarded up?"

"Not all of them. I guess they only boarded up the windows when they felt there was something valuable inside. But I can tell you this much. Every window that wasn't boarded up just isn't any more. They've all been smashed. I know some kids seem to get a thrill out of the sound of shattering glass, but this place was built for the kids. Wouldn't you think they could have left *this* place alone?"

"How do you know it was kids?"

Nelson shrugged. "Who else? By the looks of it, it must have been a whole gang of them. Whoever did this ought to go to reform school for ten years."

Ted could see some of the shattered windows himself now. It did look like just plain meanness. What did anybody have to gain by breaking the windows? Now money would have to be spent for repairs that might have meant a couple of weeks' vacation for a dozen boys.

"I thought this was going to be mostly a vacation," Ted sighed, "but it looks like we'll have to put in some heavy work."

"Yes," said Nelson gloomily, "and maybe that's not all."

"What do you mean?"

"How do you know that's all they did, just break windows? Maybe there's more to it than that. Let's scout around a little and see what we can find. You've got the keys, haven't you?"

"Not all of them, but we can check a few of the buildings, anyway. I wonder, though, if we shouldn't notify the police?"

"What's the use? Whoever did this is miles away from here by now. Anyway, Mr. Krillman'll be along soon. Let him decide what to do. Hey, you kids, stop playing with that glass. You might cut yourselves."

They headed down toward the boathouse. The younger boys trailed along, recognizing that they were faced with some problem too big for them to understand, and so they were quiet. It didn't take Ted and Nelson long to discover that even boarding up the windows hadn't protected all of them. In many cases the boards themselves had been pried loose, and the windows behind them smashed in like the others. They stopped to inspect one cabin along the way. Not only had the glass been broken, but it appeared that the loose pieces had been carefully picked away. It suggested that someone had entered through the window. They peered inside, trying to determine whether any further damage had been done, but it was too dark to tell.

At the boathouse they found there was no need for Ted's key, for the door itself had been broken in. They went inside, and Ted turned the light switch without effect. They had been told the electricity was turned on, but in this case it didn't matter, for they soon discovered that the light bulbs had been smashed as well.

"A pretty thorough job," Nelson muttered in disgust. "I'd like to get my hands on the guy who did this. If he was my size, I'd give him the beating of his life."

"And if he was smaller than you?" asked Ted, with a slight attempt at humor.

"Then all the better," Nelson returned, rubbing his hands in anticipation.

As their eyes adjusted to the dim light, they saw there had been considerable damage. The intruder seemed to have directed his most destructive effort toward the canoes. In every case the canvases had been shredded, as though with a long knife. Apparently the vandal had then taken the oars and attempted to break the canoes apart, in some cases partially succeeding. A number of oars were splintered.

"What do you think of this, Ted?" asked Nelson in a low voice.

"I don't know what to think. Broken windows make you think of young boys, ten or twelve years old. But those boards pried up, and the door stove in, and the canvases ripped, and the oars broken—no young boys did all that. It looks more like the work of a man."

"Or teenagers," Nelson insisted. "A lot of those husky teenagers are just as strong as men."

"I know," said Ted bitterly. "That's just what everybody's going to think."

"Well, don't *you* think so?" asked Nelson pointedly.

"I haven't made up my mind yet," Ted responded. "I suppose it could have been teenagers. Chances are it was. I was just thinking about that editorial I wrote."

"Changed your mind about that?" asked Nelson.

"No, I haven't changed my mind. I still believe everything I said. I also believe I couldn't have picked a worse time to say it. All right, everybody, let's go outside. No use trying to straighten up anything. Let Mr. Krillman see everything just the way it is."

In single file the boys passed through the broken door to the brighter light outside. Just then they heard the sound of a car engine approaching along the camp road.

CHAPTER 3

An Unknown Enemy

Although Mr. Blair was the official director of the camp, he was an important and busy man, and unable to give as much time to the camp as he would have liked. For this reason he had come to rely more and more upon Mr. Krillman for the actual running of affairs. Mr. Krillman devoted a good deal of time and energy to the camp, so the boys had come to recognize him as a valued friend and counselor.

In the car with the two men was another member of the party, Mr. Krillman's Airedale, Argus. The dog knew they were approaching the camp, so he stuck his head out the window and gave a few sharp barks of anticipation.

"I'm sorry that I can only stay for the weekend," said Mr. Blair, "but it's absolutely essential that I leave for a business trip early Monday morning. However, I don't imagine you'll have much trouble."

"No, I don't think so, sir," said Mr. Krillman to the older man. "In Ted Wilford and Nelson Morgan I've found two as fine assistants as it's possible to get."

"Yes, I've heard a good deal about both boys. Still, with so much work to do around the camp, I wasn't sure it was quite the best thing to have these five younger boys along."

"Oh, the work doesn't seem too pressing, and I'm sure they won't be much bother. They were all recommended by our social workers," Mr. Krillman concluded.

"Yes, yes, I'm sure you're right, since you've been in closer touch with things than I have. I was only thinking of the added burden on you. Well, I'm afraid we're going to have a hungry, accusing group of boys facing us."

He turned up toward the mess hall and stopped, noting the suitcases piled upon the ground. The boys had arrived, but no one was in sight, so he blew his horn. Presently the boys straggled into view, the younger ones hurrying along while Ted and Nelson followed more slowly. Argus, who had been released from the car, ran to meet them, wagging his tail.

"We'll have something to eat in a few minutes, boys," Mr. Blair greeted them, noting their lagging spirits but mistaking the cause. "After this we'll be on a better schedule."

Ted and Nelson came up with the group and shook hands with the men.

"I guess we've been too busy to think about eating," Nelson offered, and went on to explain about the damage. Mr. Blair's brows narrowed as he listened, while Mr. Krillman looked very disturbed. It was hardly necessary to explain to the boys that the Y always operates on a narrow budget, and there is never enough money to go around.

The men walked along with the boys to inspect some of the damage. However, they did not go all the way down to the boathouse.

"That's enough for now," called Mr. Blair. "It's done, and it can't be helped. Let's go get some supper, and we can talk about it afterward."

This suggestion, at least, was greeted with enthusiasm, and twenty minutes later the entire group sat down to a delayed but satisfying meal. The younger boys soon forgot the troubles facing the camp, and Ted and Nelson, too, were taking a brighter view. Not so the men, however, who were faced with greater responsibilities. Money and the work necessary to restore the camp were only part of the problem. Some steps would have to be taken to make sure the same thing didn't happen all over again.

"I suppose we can appeal to businessmen to make a special contribution to make good our losses," Mr. Blair mused. "I don't imagine we're covered by insurance?"

Mr. Krillman shook his head. "We're covered for fire and theft, but I hardly think that would include vandalism."

"Well, I'm sure we'll get the money from somewhere," said Mr. Blair cheerfully, "and as long as we can buy the materials we need, we can do most of the work ourselves. We'll get a crew of men and boys together, and come down here every weekend from now to summer, if we have to, until the camp's shipshape again."

"I'd hate to have to spend the money to hire a watchman," said Mr. Krillman slowly, "but it looks as though that's what we'll have to do. We have no assurance that this vandal or vandals won't be back again."

Ted and Nelson had been following this conversation closely, and felt much surprised. If the damage had been done by teenagers just being smart, it hardly seemed likely they would be back.

"You sound as though you had some special reason for saying that, Davis," said Mr. Blair, studying the younger man's face.

Mr. Krillman hesitated. "I've never said anything to anyone about it before, but the truth is I'm not satisfied about that brush fire here last summer."

"What do you mean?"

"I'm not satisfied that it was an accident. If you remember, we had a very dry late summer, and although we try to be as careful as we can, with so many different boys here there are bound to be a few who are careless or smart-alecky. However, we went through the camping season without mishap. Then, as soon as the camping season was over, and no one was around, suddenly a fire broke out."

"It was a poor time to set a fire deliberately," Mr. Blair observed. "As I recall, there were several heavy rains just as the camping season ended. The woods were no longer very dry."

"Yes, and I think that was what saved the camp. With the fire burning slowly, it was discovered in time to prevent more extensive damage. But the very fact that the woods were wet, and that nobody was around, makes it all the more unlikely the fire was accidental."

"I don't understand you, Davis," said Mr. Blair, perplexed. "If the fire were set intentionally, why wouldn't the person have set it earlier, while the woods were dry?"

"That was the part that puzzled me for so long," Mr. Krillman returned, "and because I couldn't think of a good answer, I didn't think it wise to mention my suspicions to anyone. But gradually the feeling came to me that maybe it was like this: the person who set the fire didn't want anyone to get hurt, which might easily have happened had the boys still been camping here. All he wanted was to drive the Y camp off the tract."

"But if he failed in his attempt, why didn't he try again later? He had all winter, and I believe the woods were fairly dry once more before the snow came."

"Possibly he wasn't certain he had failed. He didn't know whether we had been scared off until he saw preparations being made for another camping season. Anyway, two fires within a few months would have been too suspicious. Once he was certain we were coming back, he turned to some other form of damage."

"The Y camp isn't bothering anyone here, is it?" Nelson spoke up. "I've never heard of any complaints."

"No, I can't see that the camp is bothering anyone directly. But perhaps it could indirectly. Suppose someone wanted to use this tract for another purpose."

"For what purpose?" Ted asked him.

"For lumbering, presumably. I know that a large lumber company has expressed interest in the tract. The land had little value for lumbering up to this time, but higher prices and improved methods of lumbering and transportation have lately made it worthwhile."

"Golly, I'd hate to see the camp move," Nelson ejaculated. "We had a lot of fun here, didn't we, Ted?"

"We sure did," Ted agreed, "and I don't think there are another woods and lake as fine as these anywhere around."

"There has been some talk of moving the camp to the other side of the lake," Mr. Blair remarked, "but it would be a little less convenient, and the woods there aren't as nice. At least we can be sure of one thing. If anybody is really trying to scare us off, it isn't going to work. We're going to stay right here as long as we can."

With this Ted and Nelson nodded agreement, but Mr. Krillman was more doubtful.

"Yes, I'd like to see us stay here. But we have to consider whether the boys are being endangered in any way. If the person who set the woods on fire last year deliberately waited till the campers had all gone home, it doesn't necessarily mean he will be so considerate again. No, I'll feel much easier after we find out who did this damage and what lies behind it."

"But that's the trouble," Nelson observed. "It's hard to catch people who do something like this. It was such a senseless thing to do, and we don't have any clues to go on."

"Well, we'll do our best," Mr. Blair promised. "Like Mr. Krillman, I'll be much better satisfied when we know what this is all about. Unless we find out, we may have to hire a watchman, as he suggested. The telephone isn't connected up here. Mr. Metlow's farm on the road coming in is nearest, so I believe I'll drive down there and phone in a report to the police. One of you boys can come along, if you like. The other had better help Mr. Krillman with the younger boys, I suppose."

"Toss you for it," said Nelson, drawing a coin from his pocket.

"Tails," Ted called, as the coin was in the air. As the coin fell, Nelson studied it a moment, then without saying anything put it back in his pocket and turned away in disgust.

Ted got into the car with Mr. Blair, and they drove off. Ted didn't say much, but it was his opinion that unless the guilty party or parties had stolen some of the supplies or equipment, and were later caught with it, there didn't seem much chance that they would ever be found out. Apparently no one had seen them, or the matter would have been reported before this. Well, maybe they would get away with it this time, but if they continued, sooner or later they would overstep themselves.

Mr. Metlow was perfectly willing for them to use his telephone, and led them into the living room to show them where it was located. Since

Ted had not been asked to wait outside, he supposed it was all right for him to listen to the conversation, although of course he heard only one end of it.

"Sergeant Jeffers? This is Mr. Blair, down at the Y camp. I want to report some vandalism..."

"We can't say. At least in the hundreds of dollars. About fifty windows were smashed, and all the canoes badly damaged. We haven't been able to assess all the loss. We'll have to check the inventory in the morning to see whether anything was taken...

"No, we have no idea at all. There's nothing—

"It would have had to be sometime during the past week. We were down here last weekend, and everything was all right then...

"Well, I suppose it *could* have been just one person, although it looks more like a gang. It would have taken quite a long time to do all this damage, and I imagine one person would be afraid to stay around so long for fear of getting caught...

"No, I wouldn't say it's an emergency. It's done now, and I don't think there's anything you could do tonight. Tomorrow morning will be perfectly all right. It isn't likely they'll come back. Sneaks like that never show themselves when anybody is around....

"I'm sure we won't need a guard. We're two men, and two husky boys, and a good watchdog.

"All right, Sergeant, thank you."

He hung up and turned away from the phone. "They'll be out tomorrow morning. He wanted to send out a man tonight to stand guard, but I told him I didn't think it necessary."

"So you're having trouble down at the camp," said Mr. Metlow. "Too bad. That camp's a pretty good thing for boys. I'd hate to see anything go wrong, so you'd have to move away."

"What do you mean?" asked Mr. Blair sharply.

"Oh, well, I don't suppose there's anything to it, but there've been rumors going around that the camp would have to move. You've had trouble there before."

"Just the normal amount of trouble, I think, whenever you put two hundred boys together."

"And there was that fire, too. If I hadn't noticed the smoke in time, the camp would have gone. My farm might have followed, except that the wind was blowing the other way. Mind, I don't want the camp moved. I think it's a pretty fine thing. But with so many boys around, you can't tell when one of them is going to get careless."

"We've never had any trouble along that line," said Mr. Blair stiffly. "The fire occurred after all the boys had gone home. Incidentally, have you noticed anyone around, Mr. Metlow, especially anyone who didn't have any business here? It might have been any time during this past week."

"Let me recollect. There was only one car this last week that I recall—on Wednesday, that was, just after noon. But it didn't look like a prowler. He drove right in like he knew what he was doing."

"How long did he stay?" asked Ted, speaking for the first time.

"Can't rightly say. I didn't see him come back. We don't have many cars along the side road, but there are plenty of them along the main road. Seems most high-school boys drive a car nowadays. Some of them shouldn't. They—"

"What sort of car was it?" Mr. Blair interrupted.

"Well, let me see. I didn't see it right close up, so I can't tell you the model. But it was a new car, maybe this year's or last. And it was blue—driven by a young fellow with the top down."

CHAPTER 4

Ken Kutler Turns Up

The next morning Ted was the first to awaken, and he had time for a little walk that took him a short way beyond camp and into the woods before he was obliged to return to help with breakfast. After a tremendous pile of pancakes had disappeared, Mr. Krillman took charge of the younger boys. Ted and Nelson were assigned the grim task of helping Mr. Blair assess the damage to the camp.

They began at the boathouse. Although the damage there had been described to him, Mr. Blair had not seen it before, and his face grew long.

"That was hate—pure hate," he muttered, as he saw how the vandal had apparently tried to break the canoes into small pieces by beating them with the oars.

To hide his feelings, his manner became more businesslike. He opened the notebook in which the inventory was listed, and set about calling off the numbers of the canoes. Ted or Nelson had to locate the proper canoe, and then among them they tried to estimate how much work and what new materials would be needed to put that particular piece of equipment back into use again. At least four of the canoes seemed to be a total loss, but Nelson suggested that by salvaging parts from damaged canoes, they might be able to build two new ones.

"Remember, Ted, how we used to have those canoe-tilting contests out on the lake? You never knew when somebody was going to sneak up behind you, and kerplunk you'd find yourself in the water."

"That was the best part of the whole vacation," Ted recollected. "Even the winners managed to get themselves doused somehow."

They shook their heads a little at the thought that there was someone who wanted to deprive the boys of this fun. But their suggestion that they ought to get to work repairing the canoes during the coming week was turned down by the director.

"First things first, and I think you boys will have all you can do getting this mess cleaned up and the windows repaired."

When they had finished at the boathouse, they headed back toward the main part of camp, stopping to check several cabins that lay along the way. Not all the cabins had been entered. The Mohawk cabin and the Sioux cabin seemed to be intact, and although the Chippewa cabin had its windows broken, it apparently was not entered. The Blackfeet cabin was a different story, however. The boards covering one window had been pried off, and the window smashed. Then the intruder had unfastened the window latch, opened the window, and climbed in. The other windows, also boarded up, had been smashed from the inside, and the mattresses on each of the beds had been slashed with a knife. In this case, at least, the vandal had come fully equipped to work his vengeance.

"That took strength," Nelson remarked, referring to the mattresses. "No young boys did that."

"And he still had his knife, too, and didn't hesitate to use it," Ted observed. "A man like that might have been dangerous if he had been interrupted."

Both Nelson and Mr. Blair noted that Ted had used the word "man," although Ted had chosen the word almost unconsciously.

"Well, we don't know that it was a man," suggested Mr. Blair as he made notes of each item of damage. "I almost hope that it was, because then it wouldn't reflect upon our own boys and the good work our camp is doing. Still, it's something we may never know."

"But everybody's going to *think* it was the work of juveniles," said Ted bitterly. He could almost picture what would happen when his editorial came out. Dozens of people would stop him to ask why, if teenagers were as good citizens as he had pictured them, they had wrecked the Y camp. Worse still, a lot of adults would believe it, and wonder if it was worth while contributing to the Y camp if the kids wrecked it for themselves.

"I wish it had been a man, too," Nelson argued, "but I'm very much afraid it wasn't. It would be such a silly thing for a man to do. Why should he risk going to jail and wrecking his whole future, all over something that doesn't profit him in any way?"

"It would be just as silly a thing for teenagers to do," said Ted in rebuttal. "Why should they wreck their own camp?"

"Maybe they didn't feel it was their camp. Maybe they'd never been here, or wouldn't be able to come again, anyway. And if they ever had been here, maybe they were mad about something—you know how some people can hold a grudge for a long time over something so little it isn't worth bothering about."

Mr. Blair entered the argument. "There is this difference between a man and boys. A man would realize the seriousness of what he was doing, and the consequences to himself if he were caught. Teenagers might do something like this without stopping to weigh the consequences—might even have urged each other on as a dare. If it was a man, it was apparently a man who had completely lost control of himself. Teenagers might, of course, merely have been the wild, immature type. Well, I think we have everything here. Let's go up to the supply house. I'm anxious to know if any of our stores were touched. It might have been principally a matter of theft, after all, with all this other destruction just thrown in for good measure."

They found that the supply house had indeed been entered. Once more they settled down to checking laboriously each item on Mr. Blair's inventory sheets. As they continued, their surprise mounted, for nothing at all had been taken. The blankets and other furnishings were all intact. A great number of cartons of canned goods had been left over from the year before, but nothing was missing, although the vandal had surely passed directly by them, and could hardly have overlooked the large letters on the cardboard boxes. The supplies Mr. Krillman had brought down the week before were similarly untouched. Whatever other excuse the vandal might have had for himself, he had not been impelled by hunger or cold.

When they were finished in the supply house, they passed over to the equipment house. This was another large cabin, connected with the supply house by means of a long corridor. Since the corridor had no other necessary purpose, and was amply wide, it had been fitted up as a kind of display room and named the Trailside Museum. There were numerous glass cases in which the camp's trophies and other treasures were proudly shown. The camp's collection of fossils gathered from the vicinity had been praised by experts. A number of paintings and other decorations hung on the wall, and there were also displays of the handiwork of various gifted boys who had attended camp, and of the few Indians who still lived back in the hills. The Trailside Museum was one of the camp's most treasured features, and nearly every boy made a point of taking his parents to see it when they came to visit camp.

With the greatest relief Mr. Blair and the boys found there was no damage at all to the Trailside Museum. Since the door into the equipment house had been broken in, they knew the vandal must have passed this way, but for some reason the glass showcases had been spared.

"But why didn't he break them?" Ted pondered. "Kids who like to hear glass shattering could have had a field day here. This would have been worse than just broken windows. These showcases are expensive, and some of the exhibits are not only valuable, but irreplaceable."

"Still got a man on your mind?" said Nelson jokingly. "Just because you wrote an editorial defending teenagers, you've made up your mind to try to find some other explanation. You've crawled so far out on a limb that you're afraid to climb back."

Ted was silent. He felt there might be some truth in what Nelson had said. If teenagers really had done this, it would be silly to try to defend them. He resolved he would try to keep an open mind, until he had some convincing proof that this was the work of a man.

"The thing that puzzles me," Mr. Blair observed, "is that nothing was taken. Some of the treasures in the museum, while they are valuable, might be difficult to dispose of, but almost anybody could find some use for blankets and food and items of that nature. If this was the work of a man, he must have had a peculiar set of scruples. Apparently he thought it was all right to wreck the camp but wrong to steal anything."

"Kids might not steal anything because they'd be afraid of getting caught with it," Nelson put in. "And maybe the reason they didn't smash up the museum was because that seemed too serious even to them, and they lost their nerve."

"Or it may be they were strangers here, and going through here in the dark didn't quite know what they were passing," Mr. Blair added. "I rather think they must have come in the dark. They would figure there was too good a chance of being seen if they came by daylight."

"But then they must have had a light," Ted argued, "and a light would be conspicuous after dark."

"Yes, it might be, if there were anyone around to see. I imagine they were very careful about exposing the light, outside or near a window. Another reason why some of our equipment was spared must have been because they felt short of time. The longer they stayed around here, the better their chances of getting caught. I suppose they wanted to create as much damage as they could in a very short time, and then get out. We'll see if there's anything missing in the equipment house up ahead. That surely must have been one of their objectives, and because they were in a hurry to get there they may have disregarded the museum."

In the equipment house they found that the windows, at least, had been spared. It was chiefly the sports equipment which was kept here, and as they counted up baseballs, bats, gloves, canvas bases, catchers' paraphernalia, nets, tennis balls, and other items, they found nothing missing. At first it seemed there was no damage at all. Then they checked the locker where the inflated balls were kept, and Ted exclaimed with bitterness as he saw that every single one of the balls had been slashed, apparently with the same knife that had been used to rip the mattresses and the canoes. Soccer balls, basketballs, volleyballs, and footballs—nearly every bladder had been torn beyond repair, and in many cases the covers would have to be discarded as well. None was missing, however.

"Look at that," said Nelson disgustedly. "What kind of mind must a person have to do something like this?"

"I wonder," Ted offered. "Suppose you had been the vandal—suppose you had a grudge against the camp, maybe because you couldn't come here—would you have done that?"

"I don't know," said Nelson, shaking his head. "It would be awfully hard to imagine myself doing it. Maybe if I was good and mad enough I might cut up *most* of the balls. But I guess I would have saved a couple of them for myself, just to play with."

"Sure, so would I," said Ted quickly, "so would any boys. But the person who did this destroyed all the balls and didn't take any. That must mean they didn't have any particular use to him. *He* didn't want to play with them."

"So we're back to your man again," said Nelson, grinning. "I'm glad I didn't write an editorial, so I don't have to have an opinion. Honestly, though, Ted, it still seems more like kids to me. It all looks so wild and senseless, just like a few teenagers I could mention."

"That's just my point," Ted retaliated. "Of course we know it couldn't have been very young boys, unless they just happened to tag along, because they wouldn't have been strong enough. But it could have been teenagers, or it could have been a man or men. The trouble is that people will decide it was the teenagers, even though we don't have any proof about it."

Mr. Blair refused to express an opinion either way on the matter. "I'll leave that up to the police, and if I'm not mistaken they're probably here already. I thought I heard a car a few minutes back. Anyway, I guess we're finished in here."

The tattered balls were returned to the locker and they all went outside, the bright sunlight causing them to blink after the shuttered windows inside. They found that the police car had arrived, and a patrolman was busy talking to Mr. Krillman. There was also a third man there, a friend of Ted named Ken Kutler, the energetic young reporter for the North Ridge *News-Record*. Although he and Ken had the highest respect for each other, Ted knew that Ken was a formidable rival. As Ted's elder brother Ronald had warned him, Ken would do anything for a story, as long as it was honest and legal.

After introductions all around Mr. Blair said:

"It would appear that four cabins were entered. We've only inspected one of them so far, but in each case the vandal pried the boards off a window and entered, overturned anything he could find inside, and slit all the mattresses open. So much we could tell from looking through the window. The other windows in these cabins were of course all broken, and probably the light bulbs as well. In one instance the vandal was unable to open the window even after it was unlatched, so he picked out the pieces of glass in order to get in. The cabins were the Blackfeet, the Iroquois, the Seminole, and the Apache. The windows in the other cabins were broken only where they were unboarded, and judging from a brief inspection from the outside, no further damage was done to them. Two other buildings were entered, the boathouse and the supply house, which connects with the equipment house through the Trailside Museum. The chief damage is to the canoes and to our inflated balls. Also, the doors to the boathouse and the equipment house have been smashed in, there are some more broken windows, and shattered light bulbs. That is the extent of the damage. The Trailside Museum, I am glad to say, wasn't harmed at all."

After Ted and Nelson had told how the damage had been discovered, the group broke up. Mr. Blair took the patrolman down to the supply house and the boathouse, and Ted was alone with Ken Kutler.

"Well, Ted," said Ken cheerily, "nice seeing you again. Are we friends or rivals this trip?"

CHAPTER 5

The Legend of the Singing Trees

Ted waited a moment before answering. Ken was a friendly, sincere person, but Ted remembered all too well that Ken had beaten his brother Ronald out on a number of stories, when Ronald was a reporter for the Forestdale Town Crier, before he found a new job on a metropolitan daily. What Ken had done once, he was likely to try again.

On the other hand, Ted could hardly call himself a newspaperman, much as he would have liked to be one. He was editor of the school paper and high-school correspondent for the *Town Crier*, but the vandalism that had brought Ken down to camp had nothing to do with school affairs. If the *Town Crier* wanted the vandalism story, they would have sent their own reporter, Carl Allison, down to cover it.

"I admire your loyalty, Ted," said Ken, noting his hesitation, "but in this instance I think it's a little misplaced. Allison must have picked up the story from the police blotter by this time, the same way I did, and if he didn't come down here it's because he didn't care to. He's probably going to rely on the police report for his story."

Ted reflected that this was all quite true. Several times in the past, when he had tried to help Allison out, the reporter had been totally unappreciative of his efforts. Understandably, Ted wasn't anxious to get his fingers burned again. Besides, what did he have to tell that Allison wouldn't find out for himself?

"Then we're friends," Ted decided, "until I notify you to the contrary." Ted did not give his promises lightly, and as a budding newspaperman he knew exactly what he was promising: that he would work along with Ken as long as their friendship pact remained in effect. If at any time he saw a special story in sight for the *Town Crier*, then he and Ken would become rivals again.

"That's fine," Ken exclaimed, and seemed relieved. "I had my hands full with Ron for a few years, and I wasn't anxious to take on his brother. Now I guess I've gathered about all the facts I need. What I could use are some opinions. Although no one actually said so, 'juvenile delinquents' seemed to be the way the matter was shaping up. But I saw by the dissatisfied look on your face that you didn't quite like the way things were going. The apparent senselessness of it—like somebody letting off steam—would indicate some young hands at work. Do you see it differently?"

"That could be it, of course," Ted agreed slowly, "but there are a few things that don't quite fit in. For one thing, the person must have been very strong to do some of the things he did."

"Granted, Ted. It's a point, but not a conclusive one, since older boys might be strong enough for the job. Anything else?"

"Well, it seems to me that boys would have taken a basketball or a football for themselves, instead of simply destroying them all."

"Hmm, another point, Ted—small, but possibly important. Still, I can remember when I was a boy, if I'd come home with a basketball my parents knew I didn't have the money to buy there would have been some stern questions, and I would have had to have some pretty good answers ready. So that point can be explained, too, on the theory that they were afraid of getting caught."

"Another thing is that the Trailside Museum wasn't smashed, although you would think that if some boys were out on a smashing spree that would have been one of the chief things to attract them."

"Another good point, Ted, but it doesn't explain the point of why a *man* didn't destroy the Trailside Museum, after he went to so much trouble doing all the other damage. It's just as hard to understand one way as the other."

"One more thing," Ted went on, "is that the vandal must have come equipped with a long, sharp knife. That doesn't sound like boys who were just out for kicks."

Ken grinned. "You might have another small point there, Ted. Keep at it and they might all add up to something. So far there isn't enough to convince a police officer or a judge."

"Maybe a newspaperman?" asked Ted.

"Maybe—but just a little, and only tentatively. I've got a feeling this isn't all, Ted. You've got more than this on your mind."

"Well," Ted hesitated, knowing that they were getting beyond the realm of facts and into open speculation, "I don't know how to say it, but the whole story just doesn't *feel* right."

Ken nodded, understanding perfectly. It's all part of a newspaperman's instincts, based upon his own wide background. Sometimes all the facts seem to be there, and yet the newspaperman senses, without knowing why himself, that the supposed facts simply don't add up to the true story. Something's missing, or somehow turned around. It doesn't convince the newspaperman himself, and newspapermen are always among the most difficult persons to convince of anything.

"In what way doesn't it make sense?" asked Ken.

"The fact that it all seems to have been done without a purpose. There *is* a purpose here, in spite of the fact that it all seems so pointless. There's some sort of pattern that makes sense. I don't mean that it would make sense to you or me, but it must have made some kind of sense to the person who did it. He had some motive that seemed good and sufficient to him."

"Hmm." Ken considered the matter silently. "It's possible, Ted. But remember that when you're dealing with certain types of persons, their motives aren't likely to seem very sensible. From that point of view, it doesn't matter much if they have a motive or are striking out at random."

He went on, "Just one thing, Ted. I've heard a little about this editorial you wrote for the school paper. Are you sure that you didn't reach your opinion first, and now you're trying to shape the facts to fit your opinion?"

"I hope not," Ted replied, but he knew that Ken's advice was given in the sincerest, friendliest way possible. Such a warning, coming from an experienced newspaperman, shouldn't be dismissed lightly, and Ted promised himself to keep it in mind.

Although Ken was invited to stay for lunch, he was too busy, and declined with thanks. The police officer also left. After lunch, with the dishes done, Mr. Krillman decided that he ought to take the smaller boys into town for a movie, for he had made them a tentative promise earlier. Besides, he thought it might be just as well having them out of the way while Ted and Nelson began clearing up the broken glass.

The two junior counselors went to work at this job as the others drove off. Mr. Blair remained behind. He had a folding ruler in hand and was trying to estimate the amount of glass they would need to repair all the windows.

"I don't think I'll order it pre-cut. We can save some money if we buy it in larger sheets and cut it to size ourselves. Is that agreeable to you?"

"I wouldn't mind trying it," Nelson consented, though he could see that the broken windows were going to occupy most of his and Ted's attention during the coming week. "At that," he continued, as Mr. Blair moved on, "I'd just as soon repair windows as sew up mattresses, and I think that's the next job he's got up his sleeve."

Part of their job was to pick out the remaining loose pieces of glass in the broken windows, and although they had equipped themselves with gloves, their hands and forearms were covered with small scratches before they were through. By the time the others had returned from the movies, most of the mess had been cleared away.

"One thing I keep thinking about," Nelson stated, as they headed toward their cabin to clean up for supper, "is that blue convertible. I'll bet that car we saw on the road yesterday was the same one that Mr. Metlow saw hanging around here last Wednesday."

"Why? There are lots of blue convertibles around here."

"Sure, but how many of them are driven with the top; down in this cool weather? And there was a young guy at the wheel both times."

"All right, suppose they were the same. How does that help us?"

"Well, Wednesday was a school day, and that driver wasn't in school, although he looked young enough to be. That's kind of suspicious, isn't it?"

"Maybe he doesn't go to school, maybe he works, or maybe he played hooky. That still doesn't prove he had anything to do with the vandalism. The way he drove right out here openly, in the broad daylight, doesn't look very suspicious to me."

"O.K., then, when was the damage done? Mr. Metlow was pretty sure there weren't any cars Thursday or Friday, and if the damage was done before Wednesday the kid would have seen it, and should have reported it."

"Maybe he didn't come all the way to the camp. Mr. Metlow wasn't sure when the car came back. He might have driven in only a little way, turned around, and gone back. Besides, we can't be sure the vandal came by car. I imagine there are other ways to get in here, if a person knew his way around."

To this Nelson could only repeat his suspicions. But even if he was right, they weren't much further ahead until they could find out who the driver was.

After supper the group gathered in front of the fireplace to roast marshmallows.

"Can you tell us, Mr. Krillman," asked Nelson, remembering a question one of the boys had asked him the previous day, "how Camp Pioneer got its name?"

"Yes, I think that perhaps I can. One of the first settlers in this part of the country was a man named Homer Brintz. He believed in making friends with the Indians rather than quarreling with them. He reached an agreement to purchase some of their land from them, giving them a fair price. Furthermore, he made sure the Indians knew what they were doing, unlike other places where the Indians sold their land when they thought they were only renting it. An agreement—they called it a treaty—was carefully drawn up on parchment and inscribed in both

Indian and English characters. It is said that the treaty was placed in a heavy metal box and buried under the serpent rock, in a valley where the trees sing. The serpent rock was supposed to mark forever the boundary between Indian territory and the land belonging to the white settlers. It was further stated that the Great Spirit would deal harshly with anyone who broke the treaty."

"Was the treaty kept?" asked Ted.

"It was, at least for a long time. Homer Brintz was happy for a while, until too many settlers began crowding around. Then he packed up and headed farther west. I believe the lake was named Lake Pioneer in his honor, and the camp later acquired the same name. After he left, things did not go so well for the Indians. They were crowded back into the hills, where the land is so poor that it didn't interest the white settlers. The treaty was never found."

"What would happen if it should be found once more?" Nelson questioned.

"Oh, I don't suppose it would be of any legal significance after all this time. But it might quiet the feelings of some persons who still believe that Homer Brintz cheated the Indians and that this land rightfully belongs to them. However, I'm afraid the treaty has long ago crumbled into dust—if there ever was such a treaty."

"Do you believe this story?" Ted inquired.

"Well, Ted, I believe part of it. Like all legends, it has a basis in fact, but the facts became distorted with the passage of time. There really was a man named Homer Brintz, and he did make some sort of settlement with the Indians. I don't know whether a treaty was ever signed, and I must admit that I've never heard the singing trees, although I've come here every summer for many years."

"I wonder what they sing?" Nelson speculated. "'Yankee Doodle'?"

"More likely they sing 'Dixie,'" said Mr. Blair. "There was a light skirmish near here during the Civil War, and it was won by the Southern sympathizers. It's been named the Battle of Pine Ridge, although I think it is an exaggeration to call it a battle. You boys are probably familiar with Pine Ridge."

Ted and Nelson both nodded quickly. Pine Ridge, just west of the camp, was a favorite retreat when the campers wanted to pretend they were mountain climbing.

"Are there any Indians around here?" Joey spoke up.

"Yes, there are still some living back in the hills. They are a poor lot, living mostly on their handiwork. The white men did something worse to them than take their land. They brought them a new disease—measles.

Many of the Indians moved on, for measles is serious for Indians, and many of them died."

CHAPTER 6

Joey Sees Something

After the group was finally dismissed for the night, Ted and Nelson saw to it that the younger boys settled down in bed. Fortunately, there were enough beds in their cabin so that each of the younger boys could have a top bunk—which they considered a privilege.

"What a day!" said Nelson, when it was finally quiet. "This is kind of a weird place out here, when there aren't many people around. What do you think goes with this singing trees business, anyway?"

"Maybe it's just a story," Ted suggested.

"Kind of a silly story, isn't it, if there's no more to it than that? You'd think there must be a little something to it, or the story would have died out long before this. I wonder what the singing of the trees is supposed to sound like? Whenever the wind blows hard enough, you get a little humming sound through the branches. Maybe that's all it means."

"I wouldn't think so," Ted disagreed. "Everybody's familiar with that sort of thing—it would hardly make a very good story. If there's any truth in the legend at all, it must be some kind of sound very different from anything we're used to. That's the only way the proper valley could be identified."

"But if the trees really do sing, why hasn't anyone ever heard it recently? You know what a mob of boys there are out here every summer, and how they explore every little trail for miles around. If there were trees that sang, somebody would surely have reported it."

"I suppose so. Well, maybe it's nothing more than a story, but a good story, so why should we spoil it?"

But Nelson thought of something. "Maybe the story was true once but isn't any more. Even trees don't last forever. The trees that sang then might have been blown down, or cut down, long before this."

"Maybe," Ted answered. "I suppose, as Mr. Krillman said, the legend had its beginning in truth, until the story grew and changed with the passing years. It's like Joey's yarns."

Nelson snorted. "Of course Joey's stories have to be partly true. Did you ever try to tell a story in which everything was a complete lie? That's even harder than telling the absolute truth. But I overheard Joey telling the other kids a story today, about how he was trapped in a fire in a twenty-story building, and was rescued by firemen down a big ladder. I wonder how much truth there was in that?"

They retired soon afterward, and Ted fell asleep almost at once. Afterward he remembered the moonlight streaming through the unshaded window, and the steady humming of the rising wind.

But perhaps he did not sleep so soundly as he thought, He had a dream, which he could not later recall, that left him uneasy even in his sleep. All he knew for sure was that he awakened suddenly during the dead of night. At first he could not imagine where he was or what had aroused him. Then he saw a ghostly, white-clad figure standing by the window. A ghost? Surely not. He dismissed the notion at once, even though he felt his pulse beginning to beat faster. But if it was something more earthbound than that, at least it might be the intruder—the vandal they were looking for. Had he come back, and what was his purpose?

Then he almost smiled, as his sense of proportion returned to him. This wasn't a vandal, or at least not the teenaged or adult vandal they were after. This was one of their own boys, possibly walking in his sleep due to the strangeness of his bed. He sat up and looked across the row of upper berths. It was Joey's berth that appeared to be empty. In the lower berth opposite him Nelson was breathing heavily and steadily.

Ted got up quietly and walked over toward the window. If Joey was a sleepwalker, Ted wondered what he ought to do. You have to be careful about rousing a sleepwalker suddenly, he had been told. But before he had made up his mind, Joey heard him coming and turned his head slightly, so that Ted knew he wasn't asleep.

"Joey! What are you doing up?" asked Ted in a whisper.

"I saw something out of the window."

"Nonsense," Ted told him, for from his upper berth it would have been difficult for Joey to see anything out the window at all.

"Well, anyway, I noticed how funny the moonlight looked on the cracks in the floor, and then I got to thinking about the man in the moon and I wanted to see him. So I got up and looked out the window, and then I saw it."

"Saw what?"

"A ghost. A great big ghost as tall as a tree. It was all white and it was on fire!"

"Now, Joey, you didn't see a ghost. There's no such thing as ghosts and how could it be on fire?" When Ted had awakened and seen a white figure, a ghost was the first explanation that came to him, and so there was nothing strange about Joey's imagining the same thing. However, Ted had immediately dismissed the idea, while Joey was inclined to cling to it. "You must have been dreaming."

"No, I wasn't dreaming," the boy insisted. "First I got up to see the man in the moon, and then I looked out and the ghost went past the window. He was so tall that he had to stoop over to look in the windows."

"Did he try to look in the windows?" asked Ted. He wanted to laugh the idea away, but Joey's idea of a tall ghost couldn't be dismissed that readily. Naturally, it couldn't have been a ghost, but still...

"No," Joey admitted, and somehow Ted felt relieved.

"Probably what you saw was just moonlight," Ted assured him. "It sometimes plays strange tricks on you. Anyway, there's nothing there now. Now get back to bed before we wake the others up."

Not fully convinced, Joey was at least willing to go back to bed. He climbed up to his bunk, then pulled the covers over his head.

Ted was about to get back into his own bed when he heard vigorous, though somewhat muffled barking. This time Nelson was also aroused, and Joey cautiously popped his head out from under the covers.

"What's that?" asked Nelson in a low voice.

"Just Argus barking,"

"What's he after? Sounds kind of far away.'"

"The men must have taken him into the cabin with them. Maybe he smelled a skunk or something. Let's go to sleep."

With a grunt Nelson turned over and did just that, for he hadn't been fully awake. Ted had seen a light go on in Mr. Krillman's cabin down at the other end of their trail. He waited a few minutes, and the light went off. Everything must be all right, he reasoned, and returned to bed himself, but this time sleep did not come so quickly as it had before.

* * * *

In the morning Ted explained the situation more fully to Nelson. The latter refused to believe that Joey had seen anything at all other than the man in the moon, and agreed with Ted that Argus had probably seen or smelled some small animal. The only odd thing was that the two incidents should have occurred so close together. Possibly it could be dismissed as a mere coincidence. But the idea of a *tall* ghost bothered Ted, as he reflected upon it several times during the day. What had possessed Joey to invent a detail like that?

* * * *

They had not planned to do much work about camp on Sunday. The day was overcast and chilly, and not a particularly pleasant day to be outside. But Nelson, with two younger brothers of his own, knew how to keep the smaller boys entertained. He took them outside a couple of times for a little football scrimmage, while indoors he managed to interest them in model airplane building.

Returning from their last trip outside, one of the boys held up a small object.

"What's this? he asked.

Mr. Blair took the object and examined it closely. It consisted of three feathers, held together with a kind of decorated leather strip.

"I've never seen anything like this," Mr. Blair admitted, "but I believe I know what it means. One feather is an eagle's, one an owl's, and one a crow's. I believe that to the Indians it signifies bravery, wisdom, and comradeship. Where did you find this?"

"Down by the supply building, as we were coming back."

The director handed the colorful little decoration back to the boy. "You may want to keep it for a souvenir. I doubt that it's authentic, though. No doubt someone put it together to resemble the work of Indians."

"It must have been dropped just recently," Ted observed. "Those feathers don't look as though they had lain out in the snow all winter."

"No, I suppose not," Mr. Blair agreed. "But I don't think the Indians had anything to do with the vandalism. There are so few Indians left in the hills, and they certainly couldn't expect to get the land back after all these years."

"I don't know about that," Nelson disagreed politely but firmly. "Look how people are still fighting the Civil War. And that decoration must have come from somewhere."

Ted decided now to tell about the ghost Joey claimed to have seen. Mr. Blair was inclined to explain it as a combination of a dream, imagination, and moonshine.

"Believe me, boys, if I thought there was any real danger to the camp I'd take some strong protective measures. But I'm afraid we're letting our imaginations run away with us. There was some deplorable vandalism to the camp, it's true, but I feel sure that the boys or men who did it won't be back, and that there's nothing else to be afraid of. However, I feel confident that if anything of a more serious nature should develop, Mr. Krillman will know how to handle it, and he will be able to get in touch with me if he finds it necessary."

With an early-morning plane to catch, Mr. Blair felt obliged to leave that evening, and he drove off in the early twilight. He made some joking reference to the ghost as he left, which was the first that Mr. Krillman had heard about it. After the director had left, Mr. Krillman questioned his assistants more closely about it. Quite clearly he did not take so light a view of the matter as his superior did.

"I wonder, boys, if we hadn't better set up a guard over the camp tonight. Are you very sleepy?"

"No," Ted assured him, "but it's a pretty big place to guard, isn't it, with just the three of us?"

"Four," Mr. Krillman corrected, "counting Argus, and in some ways he's better than a man. We could each take a side, and the one on the west side would be very close to the cabin where the boys are sleeping. Let's try to pack them off early and set up our guard. I suppose it would be too much to keep going all night, but it was just after eleven last night that Argus started barking. Maybe if there is an intruder he'll come back at the same time tonight. Anyway, we can watch till midnight and see what happens."

CHAPTER 7

A Midnight Search

Fortunately the younger boys were tired out and ready for bed soon after night had settled over the camp. There was the usual bustle and confusion of getting ready for sleep, and a short pillow fight was broken up early by the junior counselors.

When the light was out and the boys settled down, Ted and Nelson went outside. Mr. Krillman had been patrolling the grounds with Argus close at his heels and now came over to join them. It was decided that Ted would guard the west side of camp, near the boys' cabin. Nelson would take the south side, Mr. Krillman the north side, while Argus would be tied to the east side, along the lake shore.

"Rather than pacing back and forth, I think it might be better if each of us would try to find some place of concealment, where we can pretty well see anything going on along that side. I'm not so much interested in scaring this person off—if there is such a person—as in finding out what he's up to.

"What about Argus?" Ted questioned him. "We can't very well hide him."

"No, we'll keep him pretty much out in the open. I'm sure he'll bark if anything approaches. That ought to make the intruder choose one of the other sides."

"Is he a good watchdog?" asked Nelson.

"He was when I got him. Since then he's been petted by so many different people that a little of the edge is gone. But I think he'll do. He doesn't usually make up with strangers unless I'm along."

The place Ted chose was a neat little cutout between two willow bushes. It was near one end of the side he was watching, so that he could cover the entire area without turning his head.

"Nobody's going to get into the camp from this side while I'm on watch," he promised himself as he settled down.

The minutes ticked away slowly, but there was nothing to interrupt the stillness other than the usual night noises. The air remained cool, and it seemed that Mr. Krillman's prediction of rain that night would be borne out as the clouds began to form overhead. That was still hours away, however, for in the east the moon had just risen, its nearly full face shining clearly.

Several times Ted looked at his watch, surprised that time should move so slowly. He was beginning to yawn occasionally now, although he wasn't really sleepy. But he didn't feel prepared to stay up all night, either, unless a crisis of some sort should develop. Mr. Krillman had said they would guard until midnight. Ted didn't really expect anyone to come. The "ghost" would hardly return so soon after its foray of the previous night, would it? Anyway, it would be a strange sort of ghost that had to be home by midnight.

A whistle suddenly startled him into full alertness. He hadn't been asleep—he was certain of that—although his thoughts had been wandering a little. Nothing moving had passed across his field of vision. Before him the little clearing that lay between the edge of the camp and the encroaching forest still lay quiet and deserted.

He listened intently, and in a moment the whistle was repeated. He recognized it as a quiet but urgent summons from Nelson, and scrambled hastily to his feet. Rounding the building on the southwest corner, he saw Nelson coming toward him.

"Come on," said Nelson in a soft voice, "I've got something to show you."

"I thought I was supposed to guard"

"Never mind that. I'm afraid we're too late already."

He led the way along the south side of the camp. About halfway, he stopped suddenly and pointed with his finger toward the back of the service building. For a moment, following his direction, Ted could see nothing. Then gradually huge, flaming words glared at him. He read:

LAST WARNING!
Get the camp
off this tract

There was a design in each of the four corners. In the upper left corner was a cluster of feathers, similar to the three feathers one of the boys had found. The upper right corner showed a group of trees from which musical notes were floating. To the lower left was the famous pirate insigne, a skull and crossbones. To the lower right was a long scroll, torn through the middle, suggesting a broken treaty.

"What's all that?" Ted whispered.

"Your guess is as good as mine. But it sure looks like somebody means business."

"But when was it done? If it was done while you were on guard, you would have seen it, wouldn't you?"

"I think so. I was moving around a little, so I wasn't exactly here all the time. But I don't think anybody could have painted it there in the little while I was gone."

"Then it must have been painted there earlier. But why didn't you see it when you first came on guard?"

"It's the moonlight, I guess. The sign doesn't glow until the light hits it just right."

"Well, it sure wasn't there during the day, or we would have seen it. It must have been painted there while we were getting the boys to bed."

"Maybe," said Nelson doubtfully, "but Mr. Krillman and Argus were roaming around, and neither of them noticed anything. He might have been able to stay out of Mr. Krillman's sight, but you'd think the dog would have heard him or smelled him."

"This camp's a pretty big place," Ted pointed out. "Maybe Argus didn't get over on this side."

Nelson, like Ted, had caught the significance of those singing trees and that torn scroll. "That must refer to the way the white men broke their treaty with the Indians. According to the legend, the Great Spirit would deal harshly with anybody breaking the treaty, but it didn't say what the Great Spirit would do."

"I'm not so much concerned about what the Great Spirit does," Ted returned, "as what some low spirits are doing around here. That skull and crossbones suggest what they have in mind for us."

"But who's responsible?" Nelson wondered. "Those three feathers must represent the tribal insigne of the Indians who think they were robbed of their land."

After a few moments discussion they decided to call Mr. Krillman. Apparently the guard they had set up had been so much wasted effort. Either someone had managed to get past them, or else he had been there and gone before their guard was established.

"You go and get Mr. Krillman," Ted decided. "I'll go back to our cabin and make sure that the boys are all right."

In less than ten minutes Mr. Krillman, Nelson, and Argus had joined him. Mr. Krillman had already seen the sign, and seemed much disturbed.

"What makes the sign glow that way?" asked Ted.

"Luminous paint, I suppose," Mr. Krillman answered, "like the dial on your wrist watch. I can't imagine, though, any more than you, when it was painted there. Argus and I were strolling not far from there while we were waiting, and I should think he would have noticed something. There are two things that strike me about that sign, though. The first is, why the vandalism, followed by a threat? Wouldn't it be more logical to have the threat first and the vandalism afterward? It says this is our last warning, but when was our first warning? The second point is that the painter of the sign would like to have us think it is the work of Indians, but the insignia indicate that he doesn't know very much about Indian lore. That crossbones is a pirate insigne, and I never heard that it was used by Indians. Nor do I believe Indians would indicate musical notes the way we do."

The boys waited silently for Mr. Krillman's further orders. That he had something on his mind was apparent to both of them.

"I'm wondering," he said slowly, "if the person who painted that sign could still be hiding somewhere in camp? With our guard established, it wouldn't have been an easy thing for him to slip in and out of camp."

"But we aren't sure when the sign was painted," Ted pointed out.

"And anyway he's had time to get away while we've been talking," Nelson added.

"Well, yes, that's true enough. He did have a chance to get away, as long as he *wanted* to get away. But how do we know that? Maybe he's still hanging around camp, maybe he has a reason for being here that we don't know anything about. I'd feel a good deal easier in my mind if I were sure that whoever was here has left again."

"I don't see how we can make a very thorough check of camp this late at night, with just the three of us," Nelson maintained.

"You're forgetting Argus. His ears are much sharper than ours, and a person who might be hidden to our eyes would be easily discovered by his nose. I'd like to go into every building in camp—just open the door and let Argus sniff inside to see if there's anything suspicious."

"That would take hours," Ted protested, while Nelson almost groaned.

"Just the same, I think it's worth the effort, if you boys aren't too tired. I know that I don't feel at all like sleeping until I know a little bit more about this business. Are you with me? I think perhaps we can do it in an hour."

"Oh, we'll go along," Ted agreed, although he had little faith in Mr. Krillman's scheme, and could tell that Nelson felt the same.

"Just you, Ted. Nelson, I want you to stand here on guard, near the boys' cabin. Ted and I will start at the opposite side of camp, and perhaps we can flush something out in your direction."

Ted understood why Mr. Krillman had chosen Nelson to be on guard, for his broad football shoulders looked formidable in the dark, while Ted was built along more tall, energetic lines.

Their plan was put into operation at once. Ted, Mr. Krillman, and Argus made their way almost in silence to the other edge of camp, and with his ring of keys Mr. Krillman began opening cabin doors. As each door was opened, Argus was urged inside. He went in, sniffed around a little, and soon came out without in any case indicating the presence of anything suspicious. While this procedure seemed adequate for the cabins, for the larger buildings the lights were switched on and Mr. Krillman and Ted also went inside to look around and in some cases walk through the building. In no case did they discover anything of importance to their purpose.

Their search took somewhat more than the hour Mr. Krillman had expected, though less than the hours Ted had indicated. When they reached the western edge of camp, they had to admit to Nelson, still standing on duty though yawning sleepily, that their mission was a failure.

"But not a complete failure," said Mr. Krillman, "for I feel better to know that whoever was here isn't still around."

He had hardly finished speaking when the air was rent with the shrill wailing of a siren.

CHAPTER 8

After the Siren

For twenty or thirty seconds the siren split the air with its mournful wail. Then suddenly it was still, and the silence seemed more deep and ominous than it had before. They waited expectantly for some renewal of the noise, but it was not repeated.

"Is that something new?" asked Ted, puzzled. "I didn't know there was a siren installed here."

"No, it's not our siren," Mr. Krillman informed them. "We've always managed with our whistles so far. It sounded like an air-raid siren, of a kind common during the war but now outmoded. I suppose someone could have picked it up at a surplus sale."

"I wonder where it came from?" Nelson speculated. "You can't tell very well, standing among a group of buildings this way, but it sure as shootin' sounded to me like it came right from the center of camp."

Both Mr. Krillman and Ted agreed with him.

"But aren't we going to try to see who did it?" Ted urged. "Whoever it was couldn't get away very fast carrying that thing."

"What's the use?" Mr. Krillman shrugged his shoulders. "We've just searched the whole camp and we couldn't find him. Even Argus couldn't find him." He looked disappointedly at the dog. "He must have sneaked in right behind us, and if he could do that, he could sneak away the same way."

"Some sneak, with that big siren," Nelson put in. It was clear that he felt let down by Mr. Krillman's lack of enthusiasm for a further search, while Mr. Krillman seemed very disappointed that their previous search had proved so useless.

"Well, I'll walk through the camp with Argus," Mr. Krillman decided, guessing their feelings. "You can come along if you want to, Nelson, but don't expect much. Ted, you'd better see to the boys. That noise surely awakened them, and they'll be wondering what happened. Don't tell them any more than you have to."

Ted found near pandemonium raging within the cabin. The boys were all awake and were in the dark except for a flashlight someone was flashing about at random. They had found themselves alone, and were much alarmed. The confusion subsided a little as Ted came in.

"What was that?" asked several voices at once.

"One of our sirens went off by accident. There's nothing to worry about. Get back in bed and go to sleep."

Not knowing whether or not the camp was equipped with sirens, the boys found Ted's explanation adequate. A couple of boys decided they wanted drinks of water, but after that they were unable to think of any further excuses, and finally settled down. Ted waited till they were quiet, then switched out the light and went outside. A few minutes later the others returned.

"No, we didn't find anything," said Mr. Krillman in reply to Ted's unspoken question.

"Not even anything to make the dog suspicious," Nelson added.

"Maybe he isn't a real ghost," said Mr. Krillman bitterly, "but he's just as elusive as one. Are the boys all right?"

"All under control," Ted advised him, and with a nod Mr. Krillman walked off.

Of course the disturbance of the night was the chief topic of conversation at breakfast the next morning.

"Where is the siren?" asked one of the boys. "I want to see it."

"I'm afraid I don't know where it is," Ted was obliged to tell them.

Suddenly the smallest boy looked very important, with his eyes wide open and his cheeks puffed out.

"Well, Emmet, what have you got to say about it?" Ted asked him.

"I know where the siren is," he advised the group.

"You do! Where is it?"

"Up there." He indicated with his forefinger toward the roof of the supply building. The top of some black object was just visible over the edge of the roof.

"Say, that sure looks like it," Ted agreed.

"Anyway, it's something," Nelson added, "and I've got a hunch it's something that doesn't belong there."

They were about finished with breakfast. The stragglers hastily gobbled a few last swallows of milk, stuffed some pieces of toast into their mouths, and followed the others over to the supply building.

There was no way to the roof of the building except from the outside. A stepladder would have been a convenience, but they were too impatient to go for it. Instead, Ted boosted himself up onto a window ledge, and with the aid of a further boost from Nelson pulled himself up on the roof. He then gave Nelson a hand, and they turned to observe the object that had caught Emmet's sharp eye.

It was an air-raid siren, all right, though not one of the most powerful kind. Rather, it was designed to warn only the inhabitants of one large building, or a small cluster of buildings or a village. That didn't change the fact that its alarm had sounded very penetrating and frightening in the small hours of the night.

"I wonder how it works?" asked Nelson, going over the instrument.

"You turn that handle, don't you?"

"Sure you do," said Nelson, giving him a queer look. "I guess most of them are equipped for emergency hand use. I just wondered if it was attached to any sort of motor."

"There wouldn't be much use attaching it to the regular power lines, for what good would it be if the current were cut off?"

"No, but I thought maybe it had a battery or a gasoline motor. This one doesn't, however. But hold on. There is something. A kind of spring here." He studied it a little longer, until he decided he had it figured out. "You wouldn't have to sit up here turning the handle to make it go. You can disconnect the cylinder, wind up the handle and fasten the spring on the catch, then re-engage the cylinder. After that, all you'd have to do to make it go off is release the catch."

"Well, that does sound a little more reasonable," Ted agreed. "I couldn't imagine someone sitting up here cranking this handle and just waiting for us to come and find him. This way all he'd have to do is release the catch and beat it fast."

Nelson was thoughtfully regarding a piece of string attached to the catch. "It looks like he had the catch tied down with this string, and if he broke the string the siren would go off. Maybe he didn't have to come up on the roof at all. He could have yanked the string from the ground and broken it."

But Ted's eyes were wandering about the roof, until he spotted something else. "Look, there's another piece of string, tied to a shingle." He stretched it out, and it just barely reached to the string Nelson was holding. "As long as he had the string tied to a shingle on the roof, I don't think he could have broken it from the ground very easily. He would have had to climb up on the roof to break it."

"Well, maybe," Nelson agreed reluctantly.

"I wonder how he got the siren up here without us hearing him?"

Nelson grunted. "Have you tried to lift this thing?" He put his finger-tips under the instrument. "I can just about lift one side, I think. A fellow would have to be a champion weight-lifter to raise this thing up over his head. I don't think one person could have done it alone, unless he had a rope and tackle, and even then he'd make a whale of a lot of noise. I'll bet you something. Nobody brought this siren into camp while we were here. It was all in place before we ever got to camp."

"Unless it was really a ghost that did it." Ted grinned.

"Don't laugh, boy. I know a ghost story that would make your hair stand on end."

"Well, go ahead and tell it. I've got all day."

"What's the use? It wouldn't sound like anything till after dark."

Nelson could not resist the temptation to give the siren handle a few experimental turns. While he didn't raise the siren to full pitch, it was enough to start the boys jumping in glee, and Mr. Krillman, who had been tinkering with his car on the edge of the camp, came hurrying toward them.

There seemed to be nothing further to do up on the roof, and the boys eased themselves down. Then they explained to Mr. Krillman about the catch and the piece of string attached, and their belief that the siren had been placed there before they came. Mr. Krillman agreed but was still skeptical about something.

"I suppose you're right." He looked about, making sure that the younger boys were out of hearing. "But I still can't understand how this fellow can get in and out of camp the way he does. Of course it's a rather big place, and there aren't many of us here, but he can't be sure where all of us are at any given moment. And there's a dog, too. If I didn't know better, I'd say it was nearly impossible he made two trips into camp last night, and yet that's apparently what he did."

"What was the other one?" asked Nelson.

"Oh, we're forgetting about that sign," said Ted, snapping his fingers. "Let's go and see what it looks like by daylight." They hurried over to the rear of the service building, where they had seen the sign, or thought they had seen it—for now they almost felt like rubbing their eyes. The sign had completely disappeared.

"Holy mackerel," Nelson spouted, "I'm glad the rest of you saw it, or I'd begin thinking I was seeing things."

"I suppose that means our 'ghost' made a third trip into camp last night," said Mr. Krillman impatiently.

"There was a shower not long after we went to bed," Ted recalled. "Let's look for footprints."

They did look carefully, but to no avail, although the ground was still muddy in spots. If anyone had passed there after the rain, he would have had to pick his way very carefully to avoid leaving traces.

"And I just don't see how anyone could do that in the dark," Nelson maintained.

"No—no more than I can understand how he got by us the other times," Mr. Krillman agreed. "The first time, of course, the time when Joey saw him, we weren't on the alert, but after that—"

"Then you believe in Joey's 'ghost'?" Ted inquired.

"Well, yes, I do believe that Joey saw something—not a ghost that was on fire and as tall as a tree—but something. It sounded to me as though it could very easily be someone with a sheet over his head— a man, possibly, but much more likely a boy. That was the reasoning, of course, behind my belief that it would be worth while to maintain a watch only until midnight. A boy getting home before midnight might find it much easier to explain where he had been than one getting home after midnight. But it was after midnight when that siren went off, and apparently much later than that when the offender returned to erase that sign, so it would seem that this 'ghost' doesn't have any special hour for getting home."

"Are we going to keep up a guard just the same?" Nelson wanted to know.

"There are only the three of us," Ted pointed out, "but at least we could set up shifts and keep one person—and a dog—on guard all night."

Mr. Krillman frowned. "Yes, we could do that, though I question how much good it would do, judging by the manner in which this person seems able to flit in and out of camp. My inclination is to give up the camping trip altogether, for the safety of the younger boys. On the other hand, we don't have any evidence that this person would attempt any physical harm against any of the people here. Quite the contrary, his objective seems to be to scare us away, and if we let him do that, that will leave him free to carry out whatever designs he has. Another point is that the boys will be very much disappointed, and some sort of explanation will have to be given. If it gets around that we've let some absurd pranks—or some real dangers—run us off the place, it might reflect seriously upon the reputation of the camp, and have an unfortunate effect upon our camping season this summer. Maybe we ought to try to get to the root of this thing right now before it grows any more serious—and I'll see if I can't arrange to get a police officer on guard here at nights."

There was very little for the young counselors to do that morning. As Mr. Krillman told them, as soon as their order of glass arrived, and he was expecting it around noon, they would all be as busy as hornets. Until then he offered to take charge of the small boys, while Ted and Nelson drove into town for some supplies.

"Will it be all right if we stop off on a couple of personal errands?" asked Ted.

"Oh, yes, take your time. I won't have any need for you until noon. We'll have a light lunch, and it won't be much work preparing it."

As they drove off, Nelson asked, "What personal errands did you have in mind?"

Ted maneuvered the car along the muddy, narrow road. He said slowly, "I thought maybe I'd better stop off at the *Town Crier* office, just to make sure they've got everything they want on this vandalism story. Of course Carl Allison probably gave them everything they need, but I want to make certain they weren't counting on me."

Nelson seldom attempted to steer him away from what Ted conceived to be his duty, although Nelson's distaste for Carl Allison showed in his screwed-up face.

In a moment Ted continued, "But that's not my principal errand. I've been wondering about that blue convertible we saw on the road Friday."

"So have I," said Nelson blithely, "wondering if I could persuade Santa Claus to leave one like it in my sock next Christmas."

"No, seriously, there was something about that car that I didn't think much about at the time. But I'm pretty sure it had a coupling in the back, the kind that you use to fasten on a trailer."

"O.K., so it was used to pull a trailer. If you'd just jotted down the license number, it would have been a lot more use to us. So what if he did use it for a trailer? How does that help us?"

"Just that maybe he rented a trailer somewhere. We could inquire about it."

"Inquire where?"

"He was driving away from Forestdale, and there's only one big place in Forestdale—Mort's Shop."

"Maybe he has his own trailer," said Nelson doubtfully.

"Sure, maybe he has, but it won't hurt to inquire, will it? And if the blue convertible we saw is the same one Mr. Metlow saw—"

"Then we're still right where we started," said Nelson cheerfully, "—nowhere."

CHAPTER 9

A Message for Ken

"A blue convertible, this year's model?" said Morton, scowling as he tried to recollect. "No, I can't recall any car like that among my customers, and I'm sure I would if there was one. Business has been sort of slack—it doesn't really pick up till the warm weather sets in—so I'd remember it all right. I must admit," he concluded with a grin, "that I don't get very many customers driving new-model convertibles. That kind of car isn't used very often for hauling."

"You're the only place around here that rents trailers, aren't you?" Ted questioned.

"I'm the largest one. But a lot of small businesses own their own trailers, and once in a while they'll rent them out."

"I've been trying to tell Ted," Nelson interposed, "that the fellow probably has his own trailer."

"Well, maybe," Morton conceded, "but a convertible is a show car, not a workhorse car. If a family had two cars, which a good many do nowadays, they'd do their hauling in the *other* one. Chances are this fellow comes from a one-car family, and just happened to find a temporary need for a trailer. Usually they can borrow one somewhere if they only want a small one for a little while. They come to me when they want a trailer for any special purpose—I've got all models—or to use for a longer time. What do you want this fellow for, anyway?"

"We just want to talk to him," said Ted with a smile. "It's kind of hard to explain."

"Oh, I know who you are now," Morton put in. "You're Ted Wilford, aren't you, and you work for the *Town Crier.* I didn't recognize you at first. Well, if it's newspaper business, you don't have to tell me anything about it. I'll read about it when you get your scoop."

"Don't count on it," said Ted with a wide grin. "I've just been lucky so far."

Perhaps Morton would have cared to argue the point, but another customer came in just then and his attention was diverted. The boys called a good-by to him and returned outside to the car.

"Well, that lead came to nothing in a hurry," Ted remarked.

"Sure, and suppose we found this car, and somehow were able to prove it was the same car Mr. Metlow saw, that's still a long way from pinning the vandalism on the driver."

"Maybe so, but at least we could find out if he saw the damage to the camp when he was out there, and, if so, why he didn't report it. If it was done after he was there, it would help us pin down the time element."

"And then where are we? Still nowhere." And Nelson began to whistle.

It had been decided that Ted would stop off at the office of the *Town Crier* while Nelson went shopping for the items Mr. Krillman had listed. Ted had reached his decision to visit the office only after some hesitation. It seemed to be going over Allison's head, and he knew Allison wouldn't like it. At the same time Ted retained a high feeling of loyalty toward Mr. Dobson, who had done so much for him and Ronald in the past, and he had no intention of letting the editor down.

Mr. Dobson and Miss Monroe were both in the office, and were glad to see him.

"I hear you are having a little excitement down at camp," Mr. Dobson observed.

"Yes," said Ted, sitting down, "and I thought I'd better look in on you just to make sure you had everything."

"I think so, Ted," returned the editor, drawing a proof sheet toward him and passing it on to Ted. "Look it over and see what you think."

Ted read the story carefully. He was experienced enough in newspaper work to tell it had been written from a police report, but it was done in Carl Allison's competent way, as long as he didn't feel someone was crossing his path. Ted could offer only two suggestions, both very minor, but Mr. Dobson made note of them.

"It didn't happen while you were there, then?"

"No, we discovered the damage when we arrived."

"That was how I figured it. I didn't send Carl out on it, since he was busy on another story. But it was a good feeling to know you were down there, for I knew you would get in touch with us if anything important came up that wasn't covered by the police report."

Then they *had* been depending on him! Ted felt a warm glow seeping through him, and he was glad he had come, whether Allison liked it or not. The fact remained, however, that the North Ridge *News-Record* had sent Ken Kutler out on it, and evidently expected to make a stronger feature of it. Ted felt Mr. Dobson ought to know, and told him.

"That's all right, Ted. It is a more important story for them, since the Y building is located in North Ridge and most of the directors live there. An editor has to use his own judgment in assessing the value of a story like this. I must admit I'm not too fond of this sort of story. Oh, we'll report on the damage, of course. But there is a very good chance that the guilty party will never be found. And if he is found, he will probably be a juvenile, and you know how papers generally are careful to soft-pedal any juvenile crime. The name of the offender must be omitted, unless there is open court action, and so on. No, it usually doesn't make for a very good story. The *News-Record* readers are likely to feel let down when nothing comes of it." He studied Ted for a moment. "Unless you know more about this story than is apparent from the police report."

"I'm not sure it was the work of juveniles," Ted informed him, and went on to tell some of the same objections he had outlined to Ken.

"You just might be on the right track," said the editor thoughtfully. "Anything more?"

"Well, we've got kind of a ghost out there, too." And Ted related some of the strange visitations.

"Well, well," said Mr. Dobson with amused interest, while Miss Monroe also listened closely. "It's not a story yet, Ted. It would only become a story if you could explain it, or it continued for a long time and caused a great deal of annoyance. But keep your eyes and ears open, for it may still develop into a story."

"Do you have any objection to my working on this with Ken?"

"Certainly not. Ken's a crackerjack reporter, but he always plays it straight. He understands your situation here, and won't take advantage of you. Let us know if anything comes up that looks like a story to you. Meanwhile, I feel that the story Carl is working on is more important to us just now."

"What story is that?" asked Ted with quick interest.

"It's a story on the trailer camp. Carl has been looking into it for some time. These people really are in a bad way. They came out here, most of them, expecting to get work at lumbering, but for some reason the lumbering failed to develop in the area as expected—"

"Was it lumbering on the Y tract?" asked Ted.

"Yes, I believe so. Carl has all the details. But these people have been hit hard. Some of them are now so badly off that they couldn't afford to move on, even if they wanted to. And they're in trouble with the health authorities, and the school authorities, and the zoning authorities, and the taxing authorities. There's some dispute about putting their trailers up on blocks and paying real-estate taxes, but they don't want to do that until they're sure they'll stay. In the meantime the school board refuses to let their children enter school. It's a pitiable situation. I'm going to see if the newspaper can't do something for them."

Mr. Dobson was puffing away contentedly, and Ted knew from experience that the editor was never so happy as when he was launching one of his famous crusades, in the forthright, fighting manner of an earlier tradition in journalism. As he rose to leave Ted wished him success, but felt it hardly necessary. When Mr. Dobson's pen began to fly, the sparks soon showered all over town. Old Crusty—as he was often called—was quite right: this was a more important story than the unsolved vandalism at the Y camp.

As the car turned into the Y road on the return trip, Mr. Metlow hailed them from his field. Nelson, who was driving, drew off to the side of the road, and they got out and walked over to the fence where the farmer was waiting.

"I've got a message for you, Ted. It came over the telephone."

"For me? Who was it from?"

"I think her name was Miss Kunts, or Miss Krints, or something like that. Do you know her?"

"No, I don't recognize the name. What did she say?"

"Here's the message. I wrote it down so I'd be sure and get it right. She said: 'Mr. Raeburn's mattress was donated to the Y.'"

Ted's face showed his bewilderment. "Are you sure about this? I don't know any Mr. Raeburn, either."

"I wrote it down just the way she said it."

"Wait a minute," Nelson interrupted. "Are you sure the message was for Ted?"

"Well, now"—the farmer rubbed his chin—"come to ponder on it, she didn't mention Ted's name. She just said that newspaper fellow down at the Y camp, and howbeit I knew that Ted was the only one of you three fellows who was tied up with a newspaper—"

Ted's brows cleared. "I think I understand now. This message was intended for Ken Kutler. She must have thought he was down here at camp. I rather think he'll be coming down soon, and if he does, I'll see that the message is delivered to him."

They thanked the farmer, and were about to leave when Ted made a sudden decision.

"Is it all right for me to use your telephone?" he requested.

"Sure, go right ahead, young fellow."

"I'll only be a minute," said Ted hurriedly to Nelson, and turned toward the house.

Finding a quarter in his pocket, he placed it on the telephone table, then asked for the number at the *Town Crier* office. When Miss Monroe answered, he said:

"This is Ted. Miss Monroe, have you ever heard the name Mr. Raeburn?"

"Mr. Raeburn? Not offhand. Do you want me to check the file on it?"

"Yes, I'd like it very much if you would, Miss Monroe. But it may take you a little while, and I don't have time to wait. Will you do that for me, and I'll check back with you as soon as I can."

"I'll be glad to, Ted. A story?"

"I can't tell yet. I'll let you know as soon as I have anything."

Then they were on their way at last.

"We're not really late," Nelson pointed out, for the clock on the dashboard showed it was still not quite noon.

"We will be in ten minutes."

"Not ten minutes. I'll make it in eight," Nelson promised, and proceeded to try to carry out his word.

"What about that message to Kutler, Ted?" Nelson asked. "What do you make of that?"

"I don't know what to think—yet," Ted responded slowly. "The *Town Crier* didn't think there was much of a story here. As Mr. Dobson explained to me, if the culprit turns out to be a boy, the story will have to be handled with kid gloves."

"That's just the trouble," Nelson interrupted. "When a boy does something like this, everybody goes out of his way to try to help him. The newspapers try to omit his name, the judge may give him a private hearing in chambers, there're interviews with his parents and teachers and everybody else, and an investigations report. Everybody's trying to help. And it's almost certain, no matter what he's done, that he'll get a chance to start over when he's twenty-one. With a man it's different. They simply toss him in the jug, and that's the end of it. Maybe that's one reason for juvenile delinquency."

Nelson was inclined to make snap judgments. For Ted, who liked to reason things through, there were ample arguments on the other side, but he didn't feel like becoming involved.

"But I'm beginning to think there may be a story here after all," Ted went on. "Mr. Dobson suggested it, when I told him about our 'ghost,' and now it looks like Ken Kutler has been following up some lead of his own."

"What did I tell you? Just eight minutes," Nelson gloated, as they pulled into camp. "Well, Ted, what do you intend doing about it?"

"The first thing I'm going to do," said Ted regretfully, "is to break a treaty of friendship."

CHAPTER 10

The One-Way Road

It would be too much to expect that Ted never told a lie. But he never lied about anything that he considered important, and he regarded his newspaper work as one of the most important things in his life. He always approached it with complete seriousness. At the time when he had made his promise to Ken, he hadn't seen a story in sight, but now that the possibility had appeared, he had to give Ken fair warning. He valued his friendship with Ken too deeply—just as his brother Ronald did—to treat it in any other fashion.

The turn of events was not entirely pleasing to Ted. It would have been fun to work along with Ken on a story. But Ted's loyalty to the *Town Crier* would not permit him to go too far along this road, for after all they did work for rival papers. Once he had warned Ken that he intended working on a story, they would each become wary of the other. The outward appearance of friendship would still be there, and they might find it convenient to help each other out for a while, but in the background there would be things they were concealing from each other. One of those things would be the meaning of the telephone message that had found its way into the wrong hands. Ted felt sure Ken intended to tell him all about it, in recognition of their treaty, but now Ted didn't want Ken to tell him. He didn't want any information coming to him off the record that he wouldn't feel free to use later if he chose.

Mr. Krillman had postponed lunch in anticipation of his helpers' arrival, and so they were in time to give him a hand with the preparations. While they were eating, a truck arrived with their order of glass, and the two boys gave an inward sigh. The load looked big enough already, and it was going to look even larger by the time they had it cut down into usable pieces. Loafing was over and hard work at hand.

They set to work immediately after lunch, Mr. Krillman doing his part by keeping the smaller boys out of the way. Though they wore gloves for handling any sharp glass, numerous small cuts were added to those they already had before the afternoon was over. For each window the edges had to be cleaned out, the new pane had to be cut, puttied into place, and the putty painted over. Then they were ready to move on to the next broken window. Days of hard work loomed ahead of them—and all for what? Because of someone's idle mischief—if that was really the only motive.

As they worked Nelson speculated:

"I wonder if they did anything about fingerprints? I know this is only a country police force, but you'd think they would have tried it."

"They did," Ted affirmed. "I heard Mr. Krillman mention it."

"Then I guess they didn't find anything," said Nelson disappointedly, "or else they would have taken our prints for comparison."

"No, they wouldn't," Ted corrected. "We're not suspects, and I've heard that police regulations won't allow them to take prints of minors who aren't under arrest—not without the consent of a parent or guardian. The truth is, though, that I don't think they found any prints."

"Gloves!" Nelson proclaimed. "Nowadays everybody's wising up. They always wear gloves, even me—ouch!" he exclaimed, for his gloves didn't stop him from picking up another scratch across the wrist.

"These cuts make me think of something," said Ted broodingly. "If we can't help getting cut while we're making repairs, what about the person who did the damage? Wouldn't you think he'd have cuts on his arms? Especially when he picked the pieces of glass away so he could get in."

"Maybe," Nelson grunted, "so now all we've got to do is find somebody with cuts on his arms. Better not tell anybody, or it might give them ideas, and you and I have the worst cuts of all."

The boys were quite willing to call it a day by five o'clock. After supper Mr. Krillman left them in charge of the boys as he drove off on an errand. Not long after that Ken Kutler drove into camp.

"Hi, Ted," Ken called, also casting a nod in Nelson's direction. "Mr. Krillman anywhere around?"

"No, he just left."

"He did? Funny, I didn't pass him on the road. How long ago did he leave?"

Ted consulted his wrist watch. "Just twelve minutes," he announced, and he and Ken exchanged quick glances, which for the moment were lost upon Nelson.

"I guess that's all right," said Ken, swinging out of his car. "I had something I wanted to talk over with you anyway."

"No, wait." Ted held up a restraining hand. "There's something I wanted to tell you first. I want to break our treaty of friendship."

"Oh." Ken hesitated. "So that's how it is. You think maybe there's a story here for you?"

"Maybe. I don't know."

"I'm sorry, Ted. I would have liked to work along with you, but I'm not blaming you. If you see a chance for a story, then that's that. I'd do the same thing in your place, and it is very decent of you to let me know how things stand. I don't know whether there's a story or not. I'm only down here because I'm following a hunch."

"You mean that it isn't juvenile delinquents?"

"Yes, and if it isn't, then there is a reason for what's happening here, and eventually we may be able to discover it and so solve the mystery."

"Did you get your telephone message from Miss Krints?" asked Ted.

"Who? Oh, Miss Carrinth. Yes, I reached her at her office." He pondered. "Was it the message that made you decide to break our treaty?"

"Yes, that and some other things."

But Ken did not ask Ted how much he knew or guessed about the message. They chatted easily about developments at camp, and Ted went on to tell his rival all about the ghostly visitations. He did this because he knew Ken would find out anyway. Mr. Krillman was under no obligation to the *Town Crier,* but only to the Y camp. He would talk to Ken openly and freely, hoping to ensure that the camp would get a good press.

But Ken did not seem too much impressed by the ghostly talk. "I doubt that it means very much, Ted, and of course I couldn't use it in its present form. It seems like kids' stuff."

"But how did he get back into camp the last time?" asked Ted.

"I don't think he did come back the last time," said Ken calmly.

"But he must have!" Ted cried. "The writing was gone by the next morning."

"I suspect that it was done by some kind of paint that isn't visible by daylight. When you look again tonight, you'll find that the writing is still there." He laughed. "Check me and see if I'm right."

The odd thing about ghosts, Ted thought, was that the more you know about them the less ghostly they seem. Maybe Ken was right about this, but it still didn't explain everything. And those threats. Just how seriously were they to be taken? In view of the damage that had already been done, they couldn't be dismissed too easily.

Ken was interested in looking at the siren, though. The instrument was too heavy for them to lift off the roof very easily, and Ken didn't feel like scrambling up on the roof the way they did, but a ladder was brought and he climbed up with the others. He noticed the obvious things they had already observed, but he also added one detail that had escaped them.

"This little catch to which the string was fastened—that wasn't the same catch that was on the siren originally. It's been replaced by someone with a soldering iron and some mechanical ability. That's what made it possible for the siren to go off merely by breaking the string."

"But why?" Ted wondered, to which Ken merely shrugged, unable to supply any better reason than they could.

When Mr. Krillman returned, Ken went off for a talk with him, and Ted and Nelson found themselves with a little time while the boys engaged in a last pre-bedtime game.

"I didn't get what you and Kutler thought was so strange—about his not meeting Mr. Krillman on the road," Nelson began. "Why should they have met?"

"Because Mr. Krillman left only twelve minutes before Ken arrived," Ted explained.

"What's that got to do with it? You can make the ride in eight minutes. We timed it ourselves, don't you remember?"

"Of course I remember," said Ted patiently, "and that's why I knew they should have met."

"How come? If this is mathematics, feed it to me slow. I'm all right about most things, but when it comes to mathematics I've got a block of wood for a head."

"All right, let's suppose that Mr. Krillman left here at exactly seven o'clock. We're convinced that under present driving conditions you can't make the drive in less than eight minutes, so Mr. Krillman reached the main road at no sooner than eight minutes after seven. Now let's suppose Ken just missed him at the main road. Ken entered the camp road just a shade after eight minutes past seven, and then Ken would have arrived here at about sixteen minutes after seven—sixteen minutes after Mr. Krillman left. To miss Mr. Krillman, Ken should have arrived at least sixteen minutes after Mr. Krillman left. But as a matter of fact he arrived only twelve minutes after, which means he should have passed Mr. Krillman on the camp road."

"Wow!" Nelson exclaimed. "I wouldn't have figured that out in ten years."

"Somebody else figured it out, though. Ken Kutler did. Maybe he never actually timed the drive from the main road to camp, but he was wondering about it, and I'll bet you anything he'll time it on his way back."

"But I still don't get it," said Nelson in bewilderment. "We've got it figured out that Mr. Krillman should have passed Kutler on the road, but Ken says he didn't. Is he lying about it?"

"No, I don't think so," said Ted slowly. "Why should he lie? Anyway, I've never known him to lie. He'll sometimes hold back part of the truth—he'll tell you that himself—but he won't lie, not even for a story."

"Well, if he isn't lying, then how come he didn't pass Mr. Krillman?"

Ted shrugged. "It must have been because Mr. Krillman wasn't on the road."

"Wasn't on the road!" Nelson almost shouted. "Where else could he be? There's only one road, and it only goes one place. And it's so narrow cars have trouble passing each other in muddy weather. Something's wrong here, Ted. Where do you think Mr. Krillman was?"

"He must have pulled his car off the road somewhere, and gone off into the woods on foot. Maybe he wanted to see someone."

"See who?" Nelson demanded.

"I don't know," said Ted with a sly grin. "Maybe your ghost."

"My ghost! You can have him and welcome to him." He clicked his nails. "Say, you just might be right. I don't mean Mr. Krillman went to meet the ghost. There isn't any ghost, and he wouldn't have gone to meet him if there was. But he might have gone on some sort of errand that he thought would help him to catch the ghost. That must be it, for sure. But I wish I knew what he was up to. We might have been able to help him, if he'd let us in on it."

"That's the trouble with most plans," said Ted philosophically. "They don't work because too many people are in on them."

"But surely he could have trusted us," said Nelson, looking very much aggrieved. "I'm not the ghost, and I'm sure you're not, either. You're altogether too solid."

"I'm not half as hefty as you are," Ted retorted.

Before taking his departure, Ken took the trouble to look up Ted once more.

"I've got something to check on," he explained, "and then I'll probably be back tomorrow. As a matter of fact, I may even spend the night here to see whether any further ghostly manifestations develop."

"I thought you weren't much interested in the ghost," Ted returned.

"My opinion, which is subject to change, is that he doesn't have very much to do with the story I'm checking. And in case you're wondering, Ted, the *only* story I'm working on here has to do with the vandalism."

Having broken their treaty, Ted felt unable to ask questions. But one thing he now knew—Ken didn't believe the vandalism was the work of a juvenile delinquent. Something—possibly something Ted had said, or a small clue Ken had uncovered—had led him to accept Ted's view of the case. Ted felt rather elated. This was the first support he had had for his theory from anyone, although others had grudgingly accepted the possibility. Knowing Ken to be a shrewd person, Ted was especially glad to have his support. Maybe that editorial he had written wouldn't get such a bad reception after all.

Following Ken's departure, the junior counselors had the job of getting the smaller boys packed off to bed. While they were doing their best with this rather frustrating job, Mr. Krillman called to them from outside the cabin and they joined him for a moment.

"Did either of you boys go into the office this evening?" Mr. Krillman inquired.

"I didn't," said Ted quickly.

"Neither did I," Nelson added.

"Well, it seems to me that someone did. The door wasn't locked, so there was no question of breaking in, but a chair was moved and a file drawer wasn't quite closed."

"Maybe it was one of the boys," Nelson suggested. "I could ask." And he grimaced a little at some of the noise coming from the cabin.

"No, please don't. If this was a serious visit, I'm sure it wasn't one of the boys. It was altogether too neat a job."

"Was anything taken?" asked Ted.

"I can't tell. The only way to tell would be to check the whole file, and that would take weeks. I suppose I'll never know, unless someday some paper I'm looking for turns up missing."

"There wasn't anything valuable in there, was there?" Nelson put in.

"Nothing that I would regard as being of monetary value. Just our camp records, in case anyone wanted some definite information. And the way it appears, if someone has been hanging around here, it may be that that information is the very thing he's after."

Ted and Nelson looked at each other. "How could a stranger have gotten into the office without being seen?" asked Ted. "Nelson and I were around all afternoon and evening, and the other boys were everywhere."

"Yes, that's just what I'd like to know," said Mr. Krillman grimly. "It looks as though this person can come and go just about as he pleases, and no one ever sees him or hears him—not even the dog."

Except for that one night when Joey saw him, Ted thought.

"If we aren't going to believe in a ghost," the counselor went on, "we're almost in the position of having to believe in a secret tunnel coming up somewhere inside camp."

"Maybe the boys could have a good time looking for it." Ted grinned.

"Didn't you say something about police protection?" Nelson spoke up. "Not that I'm afraid, or anything like that, but we don't seem to be able to stop this intruder. Maybe the police could."

"I've got good and bad news on that," Mr. Krillman explained. "There'll be a police officer on duty here tonight—I'm expecting him at any minute—so we ought to be safe enough for tonight. But the chief explained to me that he can't assign a man here regularly. That's overtime pay. If we want a permanent guard, we'll have to find the money to pay him ourselves."

The young counselors did finally manage to get their charges quieted down and on their way to sleep. When this had been accomplished, except for an occasional snicker, they felt they could take a chance and leave the boys for a while.

"Come on," said Ted urgently to Nelson.

"Where to?"

"Don't you remember? Ken said that the writing on the wall would be back again after dark. Let's go and see."

They hurried on with their errand. As they reached the back of the service building, and their eyes adjusted to the gloom, they saw at once that Ken was wrong. The writing had completely disappeared. Ted hardly knew whether to feel a little smug about catching his rival in an error, or to feel more puzzled and worried than ever that the "ghost" seemed to have made another undetected trip into camp to erase the letters.

"And it was either last night, though he didn't make any footprints in the mud, or else it was in broad daylight," Ted marveled. "Something's all wrong here. It just couldn't happen, and yet somehow it did."

"You know something?" Nelson offered, shaking his head, "I almost wish it were a ghost. From what I've heard of ghosts, all they can do is frighten you. I wish I were sure that was all this fellow had in mind."

And Ted, too, recalled those threatening words.

CHAPTER 11

The Ghost Returns

Just before it was time for the boys to retire, the police officer arrived in his car, and they were introduced to him. He was a big, husky young man who looked amply able to take care of any trouble that came his way. No mention was made of a ghost, but the patrolman had already been informed that the camp was being troubled by an intruder, and seemed grimly determined they would have no repetition of their trouble that night.

Although Patrolman Jackson looked very competent for the job before him, Ted had some private doubts. A husky policeman patrolling up and down might very well have the effect of scaring the intruder away for that night, but that wasn't what they needed. It would take something more subtle than that to catch this person who had already proved so elusive.

After handshakes all around, the officer was also introduced to Argus, who took a few inquiring sniffs.

"That's right," Jackson encouraged him. "Make sure I'm all right. After all, we're going to be partners tonight."

Argus decided that the officer was acceptable to him, and gave a few friendly wags of his tail. With that the others said good night, while the dog trotted off with his new friend to take up their stations for the night.

"Some ghost!" said Nelson with a big yawn, as he and Ted walked toward their cabin. "How many times has he been here altogether? First there was the vandalism at the camp—"

"We don't know for sure that was the same person," said Ted cautiously.

"Oh, it must have been. He was here to haul the siren up, too, but maybe that was the same time. Then he was here that night Joey saw him. I'd put a big question mark on anything Joey said he saw, but Argus heard him, too, and barked at him. Then last night he came three times—"

"Three?"

"Sure. He painted that warning on the wall, he touched off the siren, and he came back to erase the painting, either last night or today. That makes three, doesn't it?"

"I'm just wondering if there wasn't another time we haven't counted. He must have come sometime to crank up the siren and tie the catch to the string."

"Couldn't he have done that when he hauled the siren up there, or at the same time he later broke the string?"

"I don't think he could have done it before we got here, because a string stretched tight like that is likely to snap accidentally in time, especially if it got wet, and I feel pretty sure he wanted that siren to go off in the middle of the night. And I don't think he would have done it at the same time he broke the string and set the siren off, for what would be the use of having the string at all?"

"No, I can't figure out any use for the string," said Nelson slowly. "He probably wanted to touch the siren off quickly, and beat it fast before he got caught, but I don't see how the string helped him any. It would have been just as quick to release the catch directly, then drop off the roof and run."

They had reached their cabin and stood for a few minutes looking up at the sky. It was clear, but cooler than it had been for the last few days. Perhaps they were due for an unseasonable cold snap.

"Well, maybe the string was just for effect, to make the whole thing look more mysterious."

"Do you think there's any chance we might be able to trace that siren?" asked Nelson. "After all, a siren like this isn't an easy thing to get your hands on."

"I don't know, but I doubt it. If he thought there was any way of tracing it to him, he wouldn't have dared use it."

"Thank goodness for that siren," said Nelson, yawning again. "Writing that appears and disappears and a flaming ghost that runs down the road in the middle of the night are all pretty spooky. But there's nothing ghostlike about that siren. It's a good, hefty hunk of metal, weighing a couple of hundred pounds."

"And then there was his entrance into camp today," Ted continued, "when he went through the office records—all in broad daylight with everyone around. That's the thing that doesn't sound like the vandal. Remember, he was interested in destroying everything in sight. The fellow that went into the office was doing his best to keep his visit a secret."

"Just a cover up," Nelson snorted. "He's trying to do things in different ways just to keep us confused. I still think it's all the same person."

Nelson pondered for long moments. "What do you think, Ted? How is it possible for somebody to get in and out of camp so often, especially with a good watchdog on guard?"

"I think you're thinking the same thing I am," said Ted with a grim smile, "but I'm not going to say it."

"Then I'm going to say it, because it's got to be said. This idea a lot of people have that a dog can tell a good person from a bad person is silly. How did Argus decide about Patrolman Jackson? He sniffed a little and didn't notice anything unusual, then he looked around to make sure Mr. Krillman accepted the police officer. His master approved, so Argus decided the policeman must be all right, and after that they were good friends. That policeman could do almost anything now, and Argus wouldn't bark at him. It must be the same way with the intruder. It must be someone Argus already knows and has accepted. Thai's why he won't bark at him."

"A good watchdog will bark even at a person he knows, if that person seems to be doing something strange."

"Not around here he wouldn't," Nelson corrected. "There's too much activity all the time, too many people coming and going. As Mr. Krillman said, that takes the edge off any watchdog. I'm afraid if we have to depend on Argus to catch this person we want, we'll never catch him.

"But Argus did bark that one time, when Joey saw the ghost."

"Sure, but Argus was inside at the time, and couldn't tell very well who it was. He won't bark at him again—you mark my words."

After retiring, Ted lay awake for some time. He didn't feel particularly alert, having already made up his mind that the "ghost" wasn't likely to return that night with the officer on duty. But the events of the last few days had created such confusion in his mind that he found himself mulling over all the details.

Sometimes a person's best inspiration will come when he is asleep, or very nearly asleep with his mind and body relaxed. The problem is clear in his mind, but not the solution, and then something in the unconscious part of the brain takes over and introduces an idea to the conscious part that wasn't there before. So it was that night with Ted. He and Nelson had been hunting for a car that hauled a "trailer," and while talking with Mr. Dobson the "trailer" camp had been discussed, but somehow Ted had never connected the two words in his mind. He did now, and suddenly he was wide awake.

Of course it was possible that the blue convertible had been used to pull—not a work trailer as they had thought—but a real house trailer. The coupling would be the same, and it would explain why the car had the coupling on all the time. The more Ted speculated upon the idea, the more excited he became. He didn't quite believe that the driver of the car was responsible for the vandalism, but at least it might be helpful to find out what he had seen the day he had driven out to camp.

The trailer camp...the vandalism... The first was the story Carl Allison was working on for the *Town Crier.* The second was the story Ken Kutler was working on for the *News-Record.* Could it be that they were really the same story? If there was a chance of it, Ted's loyalty of course belonged to the *Town Crier.* He was glad now that he had broken his treaty with Ken, for it gave him a free hand to go after a story if he could find it.

At last Ted fell asleep, resolving that he and Nelson would pay a visit to the trailer camp at the first opportunity.

He was awakened early by the sound of a motorcar driving off, and noted the patrolman was going off duty. Once more they were on their own, and would have to deal with the "ghost" in their own fashion. Ted decided he ought to get up and see if there was anything he could do about it.

Although his watch showed it was seven o'clock, no one else was yet up and around. Ted quickly dressed and went outside, without arousing any of the sleeping boys in the cabin behind him.

He became suddenly aware that Argus had joined him and was trotting along at his heels. He stooped to give the dog a few pats on the head, and Argus responded by wagging his tail. At least Argus was up and alert in these early hours. Ted found it hard to believe that in spite of the dog an intruder had been able to go in and out of camp almost at will.

Then, looking up toward the ridge once more, Ted caught a gleam of glass—or something—catching the first rays of the morning sun and reflecting them back into his eyes.

CHAPTER 12

The Second Battle of Pine Ridge

The best thing to do, Ted thought, was to act as though nothing was happening. If someone was watching the camp through binoculars, as seemed to be the case, perhaps he could circle around Pine Ridge and come upon him unawares. No one else was yet stirring in camp. Ted strolled off, as though merely off for a morning walk, leaving camp by the south side, and then, after feeling sure he was out of sight of anyone who might be watching from the ridge, circled over to the west.

Argus remained close at his heels, glad of the chance for an early walk. He ran ahead of Ted, and sometimes lingered behind, sniffing at some obscure scent. He was not a noisy dog, though, and did not bark unless there was something strange for him to bark at. As they approached the path leading up to the ridge, Ted called him sharply to heel. After that, Argus remained within a step or two of Ted, knowing they were on a mission of some importance and that his play was temporarily at an end.

Quietly they climbed up the ridge. If he had not guessed before, Ted would have known from the dog's increasing alertness that something lay ahead of them. Argus would run ahead a few steps, and then back to Ted, his ears pricked up. Argus had heard something, or caught some scent.

Moving with great stealth, Ted mounted to the summit of the ridge. At first he could see no one there, for the foliage was rather dense. But then, some thirty feet ahead of him, he saw a form close to the camp-side edge of the ridge. He almost breathed a sigh of relief. At least this was human, and not a ghost.

Ted stepped forward boldly, knowing he had cut off the intruder's retreat, so there was no chance of his escaping without a close look at him. Thus released, Argus also charged ahead, barking wildly.

Hearing them, the person on the ridge spun around, and looked wildly for some means of escape. He was holding binoculars in his hand, which he hastily thrust into the case he was carrying on a shoulder strap.

There was no way out for him, and, recognizing it, he stood still and waited for Ted to approach him.

"Keep that dog away from me!" he ordered.

"He won't hurt you," said Ted in reply. "Down, Argus, down, boy." Somewhat reluctantly the dog held back but did not stop barking.

"Don't let him come near me," the secret watcher repeated.

"What's the matter? You're not afraid of him, are you?" Ted was closer now, and saw a boy about his own age.

"No, I'm not afraid of him. But I've been allergic to fur ever since I was a little kid. Every time I come near anything furry, it affects my breathing."

"All right, Argus, sit down," Ted commanded. When he was spoken to in that stern way, Argus knew he had to obey, and he sat on his haunches, his tongue going rapidly in and out, still not willing to miss the fun.

Then Ted came up all the way. He now recognized Woody Preston, a boy who had attended Forestdale High School for a couple of months during the winter but had since dropped out.

"You're Woody Preston, aren't you?" he asked.

"Sure, and you're Ted Wilford." Woody's tone was sneering. "I guess everybody knows Ted Wilford, the big-shot editor around school. But I'm surprised you knew me. You never paid that much attention to me while I was at school."

The boy's belligerent tone surprised Ted. Why should Woody feel so antagonistic toward him? It was true that Ted had had very little to do with him, for as editor he had been busy, and Woody had been in the next lower grade, so that Ted had little contact with him. He knew that Woody was new at school, spoke to him when he saw him, and presumed he had found his own circle of friends. Then Woody had left school suddenly, for no explicable reason. Whenever this happened it was generally assumed that the student had found a good-paying job, or else had been expelled for poor scholarship or for breaking the rules.

But that was the past. At present there was something else that needed explaining. Ted nodded toward the binoculars Woody was carrying.

"Pretty useful things," he observed. "Did you find out what you wanted to know about the camp?"

"Find out about the camp? Do you think I was spying on you? What would I want to do that for? What's the camp got that I want?"

"I wouldn't know," said Ted smoothly, "but people don't usually carry binoculars around without some reason."

"I'm a bird watcher, that's what," said Woody sullenly. "That's what I'm up so early about, and that's what I brought them for."

"Well, bird watching can be fun," Ted agreed, "but it's more customary to go along in a group. Lone bird watchers are almost as rare as a dodo."

"Who'm I supposed to go along with?" Woody retorted angrily. "I never made any friends up at school. You never went out of your way to be friendly to me. You were one of those snooty seniors who didn't even know lower classmen existed. I was there for months and never got an invitation to anything. I've been in a lot of different schools, but never in one as snobbish as this."

"Friendship is a two-way street," Ted reminded him. "If you want friends you have to take a little bit of initiative yourself. Why didn't you invite someone yourself?"

"Invite who where? I wasn't in any of the clubs, didn't know any of the places around town, and I certainly wasn't going to invite anybody over to the little place I live in. Would you have come if I asked you? No, you would have said you were too busy."

"Well, I was pretty busy," said Ted, a little lamely. "But I did try to look you up once. We ran an article in the paper giving the reaction of some of the new students to the school. I wanted to interview you, but you were out of school for a couple of days."

"Sure, I had a cold. Picked it up at school. Some dump! That's the only thing the school ever gave me. Then after I got back they couldn't wait to kick me out."

"I didn't hear that you were expelled," said Ted, frowning. "I thought maybe you'd got a job."

"Me work? Where'm I going to get a job? If you're under eighteen and don't have a high-school diploma, you might as well save your shoe leather. And when employers find out your family isn't here permanently, they won't even bother talking to you. I can't even afford to date."

"But you didn't walk way out here this early," Ted reasoned. "You must have a car."

"Sure, the family's got a car—a new one, and you know why? You can buy a new car when you can't buy a secondhand one, because the banks are more willing to give you a loan, and you don't need any money for a down payment if you've got an old one to trade in. I've got a car, but I can't afford to drive it very far."

Woody did seem to have troubles, but just how much of them was his own fault Ted couldn't tell. Anyway, they were wandering rather far from the matter that had brought them together in the early morning on a ridge overlooking camp.

"Just what are you doing, Woody, hanging around camp?" asked Ted firmly. "Do you want anything?"

"Me want anything? Not on your sweet life. And if you think I'm going to answer any more of your questions you're crazy. Who do you think you are, a detective or something?"

"No, I'm not a detective," said Ted grimly, "and I don't have any right to question you. But I think you'd better come back to camp with me and meet a person who *does* have a right to question you. I think Mr. Krillman will be very interested in finding out why you were watching the camp this morning, and if you had anything to do with certain other things that have happened in the last few days."

"If you think I'm going back to camp with you you're crazier still. I haven't even had any breakfast yet. Anyway, it looks like I'm not going to spot any more birds, so I may as well get home." He added, as Ted tried to grab his arm, "I'm warning you, Wilford, don't touch me. You can't make me go with you!"

He put up his hands ready for a fight. Although Ted had no desire for a fight, if there was no other way to get Woody to go along, there would have to be one. He was determined to clear up some of the mysterious happenings around camp if he possibly could, and he was convinced that Woody might be of some help.

Ted finally managed to grip Woody's arm, making up his mind that if there was a fight, it would be up to Woody to strike the first blow. Woody struggled to pull his left arm free, but finding he could not, raised his right fist and attempted a right to the jaw. Ted tried to duck—and now both boys discovered that in at least one respect Woody was better equipped for the fight than Ted, for Woody's shoes were rubber-soled while Ted's were not. As he ducked, Ted's feet slipped on the pine needles that coated the hillside, and he lost his balance. Woody tried to check his swing, but it was too late, and his fist landed with a crash against Ted's eye.

That was the end for Ted. What the pine needles had begun the blow completed, and he went sprawling on the ground, then rolled over and over several times, part way down the hill, until he came to a stop against a clump of bushes. He wondered whether Woody would take advantage of his fall, but Woody didn't seem to want to continue the fight. He looked after Ted a moment, saw him begin to rise, and convinced that he wasn't seriously hurt, strode quickly off into the bushes. Argus began to bark, but held his place, as he had been told.

Slowly Ted got up and brushed himself off. The fight had gone out of him as well, for he was still a little dazed and unsteady on his feet. Anyway, doubting he would be able to find Woody just now even if he tried, he decided it didn't greatly matter. They would have little trouble locating him if it proved necessary. He whistled to Argus, and headed back toward camp.

By the time he arrived there he had simmered down, although there were bruises on his elbow and leg, and he had an idea his eye was swelling shut. Woody had won this round, but that wasn't necessarily the end of it. They would meet each other again sometime, and there would be explanations, or else...

The camp was stirring by now. Nelson was outside, looking around for him, and when he caught a close glimpse of Ted's face he whistled in surprise.

"What happened to you?" he demanded.

"I walked into a door," said Ted shortly.

"Out in the woods? You'd better think of something better than that. No kidding, who did that to you? I'd almost think it was our ghost, except that what he did to your eye doesn't look very ghostlike.'

"No, it wasn't a ghost; said Ted shortly. "It was Woody Preston—remember him from school? I caught him out in the woods, spying on the camp through binoculars, and tried to get him to come back to camp with me, and this is what happened. My foot slipped—"

"Sure, I know," Nelson laughed, finding the whole affair highly amusing, once he had made sure Ted wasn't badly hurt.

"All right," Ted snapped, deciding that he would give no further details of the one-blow fight. Certainly, he hadn't covered himself with glory.

After Ted's eye had been doctored up a little, to the admiration and awe of the younger boys, they had breakfast. Other than a few remarks about "The Second Battle of Pine Ridge," Nelson did not refer directly to the fight again. He was, however, eager to discuss the new developments with Ted, and did, as soon as they had a few minutes alone.

"Say, Ted, do you think Woody really had anything to do with what's been going on here?"

"I'm not sure," said Ted thoughtfully. "There's one thing that argues against it. Woody's allergic to dogs."

"What's that got to do with it?"

"Well, we'd more or less decided that the intruder must be a friend of Argus. That isn't true in this case. Woody can't stand to have a dog near him."

"Maybe he was just pretending."

"I don't think so. He looked really worried when Argus came close to him. But whether that's true or not, Argus is no friend of his, and Argus wasn't acting."

Ted continued the discussion with his conclusion about the blue convertible belonging in the trailer camp, and at this suggestion Nelson brightened.

"Say, Ted, you might have something there. That sounds logical to me. Mort didn't think a new convertible would be used for ordinary hauling. When do we go?"

"I can tell you when. As soon as we get about eleven million more windows repaired. Did you forget that we came out here to work?"

"No, I didn't forget," Nelson sighed, "but I hoped everybody else would."

They set to work soon after breakfast, and in the hours that followed accomplished a good deal. In this respect the weather proved an ally to them, for it had turned colder, and there was an incentive to keep on the move.

"Br-r. We'll be under blankets tonight," Ted remarked, clenching and unclenching his fingers to get the circulation working in them.

"I've got news for you, buddy. The morning weather report predicted heavy snow by Thursday night."

"No fooling. This late in the season? What did Mr. Krillman have to say about it?"

"Oh, he hasn't said anything yet. I guess he's still thinking about it. The way I look at it, it wouldn't take more than two pins to get him to chuck this whole camping business and head back to town, as long as it wouldn't look like we were running away. He's really worried. I wonder what more we're in for tonight? The patrolman won't be on duty again, so maybe the ghost will have something new planned for us."

"Not if it's Woody Preston," Ted pointed out. "I don't think he'd try anything more, after getting caught this morning."

"Have you told Mr. Krillman yet?"

"No, not yet. I don't like to carry tales, but—oh, well, I guess I'll have to tell him. That vandalism is too serious to try to cover up for anybody."

At about eleven o'clock they got what Nelson considered a good break, for they ran out of putty.

"To town we go," Nelson chanted, "and maybe we can stop at Trailer Town on the way."

"If Mr. Krillman lets us," Ted added. "I don't feel like going without his consent. He's got troubles enough already."

But Mr. Krillman was not only glad to have them go, but had a list of supplies of his own that he wanted them to pick up. They did not explain all their reasons for wanting to stop at the trailer camp, merely stating that they wanted to see someone there, and he gave his consent, hoping they would get back soon after noon. Ted also told him all he knew about Woody Preston, and although the counselor noted the name, he didn't have much to say about Ted's eye, feeling it was a matter Ted could handle for himself.

The boys drove off. There was no argument about who should drive, for Ted had trouble seeing out of his left eye, and willingly surrendered the wheel. But though they were in a hurry, Ted asked Nelson to drive very slowly.

"What for?" Nelson wanted to know.

"Because I'm looking for something." A few minutes later Ted called, "Stop here."

Nelson stopped the car, and they got out. "What's up?" he demanded.

"Look here, on the ground. Tire tracks. This is where Mr. Krillman stopped his car last night, so that Ken didn't see him. He drove right off the road, and the car was hidden behind these bushes. I wonder what he was after?"

They looked around them. There was nothing but woods. No further the tracks showed, so there could not have been another car. And there was no habitation around. If Mr. Krillman had come out here to meet someone, he had met him alone out in the woods.

But whether he had actually come to meet the ghost, or to set up some sort of trap that he thought might capture the ghost, they couldn't decide, and finally drove on without having cleared up one more mystery.

CHAPTER 13

Tin-Can Tourists

At the trailer camp they found a hundred-odd house trailers lined up in neat rows and sections suggesting city blocks. Some of the campers had even tried to stake out little yards, and early spring flowers were just beginning to push through. In one respect, however, this camp differed from many other trailer camps, for all the trailers stood on tires, rather than on blocks which is usually done when the campers intend to settle down for a while. However temporary their stay, they seemed to be doing their best to make their surroundings decently livable, and they hardly deserved the term "tin-can tourists" which was often applied to them, either because so much of their food came from tin cans or because the trailers themselves were being compared unfavorably with sardine cans.

Ted and Nelson had no trouble locating the blue convertible they were after. The first person they asked said:

"Oh, you must mean the Preston car. That's their home, the next street over and the third house from the corner."

"Well!" Nelson exclaimed to Ted as they started on foot toward the Preston "house," "all roads seem to lead to Woody Preston. He'll think we showed up here because of his fight with you, and we didn't at all. We came the long way around."

"I wonder why I didn't guess that he lived at the trailer camp? He gave me enough clues, about his family not being settled down here permanently and all that. And he wasn't expelled from school, as I thought. Mr. Dobson told me that the school board and the trailerites were having a dispute over the payment of tuition fees, and that's why the school decided not to admit him. That makes it pretty hard on him and the other students here."

"Do you think Woody has anything to do with this ghost business?"

"Well, if he's the driver of that blue convertible, we know he's been hanging around camp for something more than watching birds. He doesn't like us, so probably he doesn't like the camp, either, but what else he's got in mind I can't guess."

Mr. Preston answered their knock, and seemed pleased to see them.

"It isn't very often that Woody brings his friends around here. I wish he would. I'm sorry that he isn't at home just now. He's off with his crowd somewhere."

Woody's father evidently believed his son had a group of friends with whom he went around, but Woody had already denied it to Ted.

"He drives a blue convertible, doesn't he?" asked Ted.

"Oh, yes. I suppose I really shouldn't have bought a new car. But I thought lumbering would be opening up around here long before this. And it gave Woody something to do. He hasn't had much to fill his time since he left school."

"It's too bad about that," Ted offered, "just when he was beginning to get acquainted around school. His grades were all right, weren't they?"

"Yes, he did all right. I won't say he's too much of a scholar, but he shines along mechanical and scientific lines. That's why I'm anxious for him to finish high school and perhaps go on to college. He's a year behind for his age, due to the way we've been moving around."

Mr. Preston spoke of his son with much pride and affection, and it was clear that if Woody had been up to anything out at camp, his father knew nothing about it. The boys decided not to try to question him any further and left to do their errands. They still had to pick up the necessary supplies for camp, and Ted asked Nelson if he could manage them by himself.

"Sure. But what are you going to do?"

"I want to call the newspaper, and I didn't like to call from Mr. Metlow's. Miss Monroe is checking into that Mr. Raeburn business for me."

Miss Monroe was expecting his call, and had some information for him.

"Yes, Ted, I found the name in our files. In fact, I recollected something about the story after I had refreshed my memory from the clippings. It was a fairly big story a number of years back, so that I'm surprised I'd forgotten.

"Mr. Raeburn was a farmer, quite old, and had lived all by himself for many years. There had been various housekeepers and hired men, but he always managed to quarrel with them, so they never stayed very long. He'd also quarreled with most of his neighbors, so they left him pretty much to himself. There were also quite a number of relatives, but they never came to visit him, for the same reason. It seemed that it was just impossible for anyone to get along with him. Perhaps he wasn't quite rational.

"In some way or other the rumor developed and was widely circulated that Mr. Raeburn was very wealthy. Certainly there was no evidence of it about the farm, for he lived very frugally, and the place was considerably run down and the livestock poor. But this did nothing to stop the rumors, for it was claimed he was hoarding all his money and that it was hidden somewhere on the farm. While it is true that he never spent much money, whether he was wealthy or not was never proved. Maybe he never spent anything because he didn't have it. But if he was indeed wealthy, there was a very good chance that his wealth consisted of cash, and was concealed somewhere about, for he had a mistrust of banks, just as he mistrusted most people.

"When he became very ill, a neighboring couple, Mr. and Mrs. Parsons, decided that they would have to take care of him, whether they cared very much for him or not, and after that one or the other was generally about the place, up until the time Mr. Raeburn died. Mr. and Mrs. Parsons claimed to be motivated only by reasons of charity, but a good many people later thought the couple had been seeking some clue to where he had hidden his money.

"After Mr. Raeburn died, the place was cleaned up, but no money was found, and there seemed to be little reason to believe the old rumors. Then unexpectedly it was discovered that Mr. Raeburn had held a safe-deposit box in the local bank. It was opened by court order, and it was widely expected that the money would at last be found, but all it contained was a will, of which no one had had previous knowledge. The will made his nephew, James Hardy, his sole heir. Specifically, it said that his beloved nephew, James Hardy, was to assume all his possessions, including $18,000 in cash. This was the first definite mention of any money, and created considerable excitement among the remaining relatives who hoped to break the will. The oddest thing about the will was that James Hardy should have been named heir, for he was the relative with whom Mr. Raeburn had quarreled the most bitterly. Some said that Mr. Raeburn was sorry for the way he behaved toward his nephew, and wanted to make amends.

"Of course the heirs went over the farm with a fine-tooth comb, but the money was not found. When all searches failed, the next obvious thing was to wonder whether the money could have left the farm before Mr. Raeburn died. Naturally, this threw suspicion upon Mr. and Mrs. Parsons, and they were questioned closely."

Here the operator interrupted, and Ted dropped another dime into the slot. Miss Monroe continued:

"Mr. and Mrs. Parsons denied knowing anything about the money. Upon further questioning, they did admit they had sold some old furniture from the attic to a secondhand dealer to meet Mr. Raeburn's expenses. They claimed they had done this only on Mr. Raeburn's orders.

The opinion developed among the relatives that perhaps the money had been concealed in the furniture, for the couple didn't think to examine it very carefully."

"Mr. Raeburn wouldn't have ordered them to sell the furniture if the money was concealed there, would he?" Ted questioned.

"You wouldn't think so, would you? But there are other possibilities. Perhaps Mr. Raeburn was so ill that he didn't quite know what he was doing. Or perhaps Mr. and Mrs. Parsons sold the furniture without his knowledge, only claiming afterward they had his consent when they learned it might have been valuable. But I believe it was Ken Kutler who had another theory about the whole affair. He thought the money was really in the furniture, and that Mr. Raeburn deliberately had it sold, as a last bitter joke upon his nephew. If his nephew was able to find the money—well, all right, but Mr. Raeburn wanted to make things difficult for him. Perhaps he hoped his nephew would never find the money, or, if he did, would be unable to claim it, and then would always regret the way he had treated his uncle. Few people who knew Mr. Raeburn actually believed he would have blamed himself for the quarrel."

"Wasn't the furniture dealer questioned?" Ted interrogated.

"No, it was an itinerant dealer who was never found. Naturally, this didn't help the couple's story any, and some people, especially the relatives who were very bitter about the whole thing, believed that no furniture was ever sold, and that the couple found and appropriated the money. Since that time they have lived under a shadow. While no one can prove they didn't take the money, they certainly haven't been spending it, but are still living in the same humble fashion."

After a few more questions Ted hung up, feeling more puzzled than ever by this new turn of events, although he realized the water was running much deeper than he had guessed. What did Ken Kutler suspect about the missing money? Had he really tracked it down to the Y camp, and what did that have to do with the vandalism?

Ted was in time to help Nelson load up the car with the supplies he had purchased. While doing it, Ted managed to tell him most of the details he had learned from Miss Monroe. Nelson was at first skeptical.

"How do you know there really was any money, Ted? Mr. Raeburn might have made the whole thing up."

"Yes, I thought of that, too, and asked Miss Monroe. She said that most people who knew him didn't think so. He was known to be very blunt and very truthful—which is maybe why he didn't have any friends. If he said he had the money, he probably did, but he didn't want it to be found very easily."

"Say, wouldn't it be something if we could find the money? That would help the camp out a lot. Or whose money would it be?"

"Let's worry about that after we find it," said Ted practically.

"Yes, but I wonder. Ken seems to think the money was hidden in a mattress that may have found its way to the Y camp. But say, what about all those slashed mattresses? Do you think the vandal was really after the Raeburn money?"

"I don't know what to think, but I think that's what *Ken* thinks."

"He might be right, because he's always got a lot on the ball. But if the vandal was after the money, he probably found it, and so what do we do now?"

"I don't know the answer to that, either," said Ted patiently. "But the way I figure it, Ken must know a lot more about it than we do, so let's wait and see what he does next. Meanwhile, not a word to anybody."

Nelson frowned. "But if the mattress did get here somehow, how did Ken find out about it? Nobody else was able to locate it."

"Maybe because they were working from the wrong end," Ted explained. "They couldn't trace the mattress from the farm to the camp, because the itinerant secondhand dealer couldn't be found. But working from the Y records and tracing backward, Ken may have been able to locate it. Come to think of it, Miss Carrinth is a Y secretary, isn't she, and she was the one who sent Ken that message."

Nelson was considering all the details in his orderly mind. "Now if the vandal knew about the Raeburn mattress, and that was what he was after, why did he do all the other damage?"

"To make it look like the work of juvenile delinquents, of course."

"O.K., I'm with you so far. But did he know which mattress it was? If so, why didn't he just go to that one mattress?"

"Maybe the same thing—so it would look like mere random destruction."

"Maybe—but I'm thinking of something else. Maybe he didn't know for sure just which mattress it was, and just kept going. Maybe," said Nelson in sudden excitement, "it's still here!"

"Sure, and maybe he just kept going until he found what he wanted, and now it's gone," said Ted, more practically. "We'll just have to wait and see what the future brings. You know something funny, though. From the very beginning, when we found the mattresses slashed, the thought came to me that maybe something was hidden there. Later, when we heard about the missing treaty, I had a quick idea maybe that was it."

"A treaty more than a hundred years old?" asked Nelson skeptically. "Some of these mattresses are pretty old, but I don't think any of them are *that* old."

"I don't mean that the treaty was there for a hundred years. Maybe somebody just put it there lately as a hiding place."

Nelson didn't think much of the idea. "If that treaty were to last for a century, it would take some pretty delicate handling, I'll tell you. Putting it in a mattress, and having somebody roll on it a few times, would crumble it into dust. Chances are that's what happened anyway, long before this. If there ever was a treaty—and if anybody ever found it. Say, is my stomach fast, or are we late for lunch?"

"We're late. Your stomach seems to be right on time."

CHAPTER 14

Joey's Story

As they drove into camp, the place seemed deserted. Even Argus, who was usually on hand to greet every new arrival, had disappeared.

"Where is everybody?" Nelson demanded, after giving a few calls to which there was no response.

"Probably in the mess hall. Let's try there."

The door to the mess hall was unlocked, but there was no one inside. They stood for a moment, puzzled by the strange silence.

"Maybe Mr. Krillman's in his office," Ted suggested. "He mentioned that he had a little work he wanted to do."

"Sure, if you can get any work done with five boys prancing around. Maybe they went out for a hike."

"At lunchtime?"

"Maybe they took lunch with them. Or maybe they were delayed getting back."

They decided to try the office, though, and although no one was there, they found a note on the door that explained the situation to them. Ted read the note aloud:

"'Joey has wandered off, and we are out looking for him. We will try north and move toward the northeast, because the boys think he went looking for Indians. If you get back in time, try the northwest. But return to camp about one, and if we don't find him by then we'll organize a full-scale search.'"

"Joey again! Wow!" Nelson exclaimed. "For his size, that kid's just about the biggest nuisance I've ever come up with."

"I suppose you can't blame him very much for wanting to see Indians," Ted offered.

"No, I guess not, but if he's lost in these woods, and isn't found before dark, things aren't going to be very funny. I wonder if Argus is with him? That way it wouldn't be so bad."

Ted zipped up his jacket and pulled on his gloves as well. Earlier he had worn them for protection from the glass, but now he was wearing them because of the increasing chill in the air. No, they didn't have any time to lose, especially if the weatherman was right in his prediction of colder weather.

"Northwest?" said Nelson, trying to orient himself with the territory they were expected to explore. "The campers never hiked very much in that direction. There's a big dead-end ravine there and a lot of barbed-wire fences on the other side where the farming begins."

They were moving along with rapid strides. "Maybe the barbed wire keeps the livestock in, but it doesn't always keep human beings out," Ted stated. "Joey just might try to get through."

"I wonder if he could, though, Ted, counting the ravine, too. It would be pretty tough for a little kid like that, unless he found a path, and I don't think there's very much in the way of paths."

"I don't know about Joey," Ted returned, "but we'll see if we can't find it. If Joey came this way, he must have taken either the road or a path, and we didn't see him on the road."

"Unless he was hiding from us."

"If he was hiding from us," said Ted grimly, "we've got one sweet job on our hands."

They skirted along the edge of the ravine, looking for a way down. There was little to attract hikers in this direction, for the hill was steep and densely covered with underbrush, and it was rather marshy down below, while experienced hikers would know that the ravine didn't lead anywhere anyway. But it was fairly long, and at the upper end divided into a number of branches, so that it wasn't easy to circle it.

"Hold on!" Nelson exclaimed. "This looks like a little path here. I don't remember ever seeing it before, do you?"

"Search me! I haven't been out this way for years."

"Well, I don't see any other path going down, and it looks like things are going to get worse if we go on up here. Let's go down this path and see what happens."

"All right," Ted agreed, having no alternate plan, "but I don't see any path leading up the other side, and that marsh doesn't look very attractive."

At the bottom of the hill they found things a little better than they had expected. The ground was not quite so soft as it looked from above, and they found that the path twisted skillfully around the worst spots. It led them along the bed of the valley through which a stream must have flowed at one time but was now quite dry. After a short distance, they turned a bend, and then unexpectedly the path led up the opposite hillside—not too steep for them to make it, but steep enough to keep them scrambling and panting for breath.

"I don't know about Joey, though," Ted remarked.

"He's a sturdy little kid. I think he could make it all right, but the way the path is hidden, I don't think it's very likely he found it. Want to go on?"

"We may as well," Ted decided. "We won't have time to look anywhere else before one o'clock. Hold it. What's that over there?"

Nelson stopped, and followed Ted's glance. "It looks like a crevice among the rocks. Maybe it's a small cave. It might be just the sort of thing a boy would crawl into for shelter. Let's go and see."

"Take it easy," Ted advised. "It looks like something in there, but I don't know whether it's Joey. Maybe it's an animal of some kind, and you know what a cornered wild animal is like. White, though. What's white at this time of year?"

"A rabbit's tail or a skunk's backbone," Nelson informed him.

They were at the opening of the cave by now. Stooping, Ted peered cautiously inside. Then he laughed, and reached in his hand. Whatever he drew out wasn't alive. It was a large bedsheet wrapped about something long and narrow.

"We didn't find Joey, but we found Joey's ghost," said Ted with satisfaction. "Just a sheet, with some small holes in it to see through, and a pair of long stilts! No wonder Joey said the ghost looked as tall as a tree!"

"So that little pest was telling the truth all the time," said Nelson in admiration. "I take back everything I said about him—anyway, most of it. Isn't there something queer about that sheet, Ted? It looks sort of funny."

"Yes, it's got something on it. I can feel it with my hands." He thought about it a moment, then suddenly thrust the sheet back into the hole. There could be no question now that the sheet looked brighter than it should have in the dark.

"What do you know? Luminous paint," said Nelson in awe. "So Joey was right about that, too, and the ghost did look on fire to him."

"Yes, the same kind of paint, probably, that was used to paint that warning on the wall. Well, we know something for sure now. There was a ghost, and this is the secret path by which he reached camp, and somebody is trying to scare the camp off this tract."

"But we still don't know who or why, or how he was able to get in and out of camp so often." They stared in silence for a few moments. "Well, what do we do now, Ted, take this stuff with us?"

"No, let's put it back. There's no use alarming the ghost. And important as all this is, it's not so important as finding Joey. I don't think he came this way, but let's climb all the way to the top of the hill and see what we can see."

The path led around a kind of scar on the hillside, as though there had been a small landslide there sometime during the past year, and the vegetation had not yet grown back. Some of the odd-colored rocks that had been uncovered caught Ted's eye, and he stooped to pick up a few.

"Kind of unusual," he remarked, holding them up to the light for inspection. "I think I'll take a few back for the boys' rock collections. They were talking about them the other day but haven't been able to get much along that line so far."

As he placed the stones in the pocket of his jacket, a voice hailed them from above.

"Hey, there! What are you boys doing? Don't you know this is private property?"

A man stood at the top of the hill, a farmer wearing a yellow-checked hat. It wasn't Mr. Metlow, and so by inference they decided it must be Mr. Thompkins, who owned the next farm.

"Let's go up and talk to him," Ted whispered. "We might find out about Joey."

"All right," Nelson grumbled. "I don't suppose he'll eat us up, although he looks like he might like to."

As they reached the hill's crest, gradually clearing fields opened up in front of them. The path they had been following led directly to a barbed-wire fence, and they could tell that someone had grown used to going through there, for one strand was pulled loose. However, they had no opportunity to follow the path even if they had wished, for the farmer stood directly in their way.

"Mr. Thompkins?" Ted asked. "We're from the camp. We're out looking for a little boy who wandered off, and wondered if he came this way."

"No, he didn't. That I'm sure of. If he did, you can be sure I'd send him packing back to camp in short order. I don't like to seem rude, but last summer some of you boys left my fence open, and three of my cows wandered off and nearly fell into the ravine."

"We're sorry," Ted apologized. "The boys have strict orders about that."

"I don't care about their orders," the farmer grumbled. "I just wish they'd stay away from here. Now I see they've worn a path through my property. Be kind to them once and they'd soon walk off with the whole place."

"We thought the path led to Mr. Metlow's farm," Nelson remarked.

"No, it runs right between our farms most of the way, and you can see there how it cuts across my back pasture. I thought the idea of camps like yours was a place for boys to go so they wouldn't be bothering the rest of us."

They had no answer to, that. The farmer went on:

"You sure you boys are from the camp? Yes, I suppose you are. But there's been somebody else hanging around here. I've seen him three or four times, and I can't imagine what he's up to."

"A boy?" asked Ted.

"No, a man, big, heavy, wearing a long overcoat. You got a man like that over at your camp?"

"No, the description doesn't fit either of our directors. We're sorry if we've bothered you, Mr. Thompkins, but we're anxious about Joey."

"Well, if it wasn't somebody from camp, I suppose it's the tax assessor. There's always something."

The farmer grumbled some more, which they took to be a sort of half-apology, and then they left him.

"I don't think that man likes us," Nelson decided.

"Maybe you wouldn't be so gracious, either, if it were your cows that almost fell in the ravine."

They retraced their steps across the ravine, and made good time on the way back toward camp. They had covered more than half the distance when they noticed someone up ahead of them. It was a man who was a stranger to them, although they knew at once he fitted Mr. Thompkins' description. Hearing them coming, he gave them a casual glance but did not appear at all disturbed. Instead, he went calmly about his job of studying, and occasionally measuring, some of the trees around him...

Ted hailed him. "Did you see a little boy, about so high, wandering around here? He may have had a dog with him."

"No, no little boy, and no dog, either." The man was not unfriendly, but he didn't appear particularly anxious to be friendly, either. He made no effort to introduce himself or explain his business.

"Have you been here long?" Ted questioned him. "We're sorry to bother you, but we're anxious to find the boy before he really gets good and lost."

"I've been here about two hours, and he hasn't passed in that time. I hope you find him. This is a pretty big wood to get lost in."

"You must have come in by this trail," Nelson observed, "and through the barbed-wire fences."

"That seems to be the only way of getting here," said the man coolly, "except round by the road. The path looked well used, so I didn't think anyone would mind."

And still he made no attempt to explain his business there. The boys didn't like the idea of a stranger hanging about camp, but still he seemed to know what he was doing, and they supposed he probably had as much right to be there as they had.

"Well, if you should see the boy, be sure and send him back to camp," Ted urged.

"You can be sure I'll see that he gets there all right. I've got three youngsters of my own." The man turned away, and there was nothing more they could do but go on their way.

"Anyway, I'm pretty sure that's not our ghost," Nelson remarked. "As heavy as he is, he'd never have been able to get on those stilts. He must weigh about two hundred and fifty pounds."

"I wonder if Mr. Thompkins could have known about the ghost's things in the cave?" Ted pondered. "It's on his property. I don't suppose he did, though. It's right at the end of his farm, so I don't imagine he gets down that way very often."

They arrived at camp to find it as deserted as they had left it. It didn't look as though the other party had had any better luck at finding Joey than they.

"Now what?" asked Nelson, beginning to fidget, for inactivity or indecision was always irritating to him.

"We may as well wait at the mess hall," said Ted dully. He felt very depressed, for he had half-hoped and expected that Mr. Krillman would be successful in finding Joey. Up until now he hadn't really been worried.

"Wait a minute, though," Ted added. "Let's stop by our cabin. I want to check Joey's clothes."

"What for?"

"It might help to know what he was wearing, and it will relieve my mind a little to know that he was properly dressed for this cold weather. But that's not all. We can see if he took everything with him. If he did, it means either that he ran away, or that he got homesick and started for home. If he left the rest of the things, then that means he intended to come back."

Then, suddenly, there was a scuffling behind them, and Argus leaped madly upon them, wagging his tail with great vigor and trying to lick their faces.

"All right, good dog, down, boy," said Ted, patting him on the head. "Where did you come from, anyway? You weren't here before."

"Maybe he ran in ahead of the others," Nelson suggested.

They went on to their cabin, Argus trailing behind them, and were surprised to find the door slightly ajar. They were just in time to catch Joey sitting up in bed, stretching, and rubbing his eyes! They ran to him in excited relief.

"Joey! Where were you?" Ted questioned.

"I—guess I was asleep," he answered lamely. He was still wearing his jacket, scarf, and rubbers, along with one mitten, the other having fallen off on the floor.

"I know you were asleep, but how long were you asleep, and where were you before that?"

"I don't know how long I was sleeping. But before that I went with Argus, because we wanted to look for Indians."

"Did you find any?" Nelson interjected.

"No." He shook his head. "Maybe it was too early in the spring and they hadn't come back yet." The older boys looked puzzled at this. Joey seemed to think the Indians migrated, like the birds, but they did not try to correct him.

"Well, when did you get back?" Ted asked him.

"Just before I went to sleep," Joey explained, and it was clear this was as much as he would be able to tell them. "There wasn't anybody around, and I was tired, so I wanted to sleep for a while. I told the man I was tired, and he said it would be a good idea for me to go back to camp and take a nap."

"What man?" Nelson wanted to know, while Ted looked at him significantly. Could it be the same man they themselves had seen in the woods? That hardly seemed possible, for he had denied seeing Joey, and they had believed him.

"I don't know," Joey replied. "He wasn't very nice to me. He said I ought to get a spanking for wandering so far away from camp."

"Not a bad idea at that," Nelson retorted. "You ought to be glad he found you at all."

"What did he look like?" Ted questioned. "Was he short and fat?"

"No, he wasn't very fat, and he was tall."

"As tall as the ghost?" asked Nelson jestingly.

Joey considered. "No, not that tall. But he looked funny because he was wearing orange glasses."

Sunglasses are common during the summer or during the bright snow of winter, but they were unusual for that time of year. Could Joey have imagined it?

"Maybe the man has weak eyes," said Ted to Nelson in a low voice.

"If there was a man," Nelson replied. "Where did the man stay?" he questioned Joey.

"In a cabin up on the hill."

The boys were all attention. It was true that there were a number of cabins scattered around through the hills, and it was possible that one or more of them might have been inhabited, but they hadn't heard of anyone living close enough to the camp for Joey to find him.

"Where was the cabin?" asked Ted, watching Joey closely. He had not been very successful in trying to discover when Joey was lying, but that didn't stop him from trying.

"That way," said Joey, nodding vaguely toward the south, and Nelson sighed a little in exasperation. The hills were to the north, and it didn't seem likely Joey had gone south. "It was near the valley where we heard the trees sing, and I got scared, and Argus barked, and then the man came and asked us where we belonged, and he showed us the way home."

"The trees sing!" Ted exclaimed, while Nelson added:

"This kid's lying. He's heard us talking about the singing trees, and now he imagines he's heard them himself."

"I'm not lying," said Joey firmly.

"All right, Joey," said Ted quietly, for Joey was becoming excited, "we don't think you're lying, but maybe you don't quite remember exactly what happened. If you heard the trees sing, what did they sound like?"

Joey groped for words to express himself. "They sounded sort of like an orchestra, only I couldn't tell what they were playing. It got louder and softer, and then it went up and down, and I couldn't see any orchestra and I got scared, and then Argus began to bark—"

"That's all right, Joey, if you say you heard the trees sing, then maybe you did. We won't talk about it any more till Mr. Krillman gets back. Maybe," he added as Argus suddenly dashed out of the cabin, "they're coming now."

Joey got up and dried his face, and left the cabin ahead of them.

"Another strange thing," Ted remarked to Nelson. "Do you think the singing trees could have anything to do with the 'ghost' that's been hanging around here?"

"If you want to know what I think," said Nelson firmly, "I think Joey made the whole thing up. He got tired playing baseball with the other boys this morning, and came in here and took a nap, and has been here all the time."

"Argus wasn't here before."

"Maybe he was out chasing rabbits."

"But Joey even told us what the man looked like."

"That doesn't mean anything," Nelson argued. "When I was little I had an imaginary playmate, and I named him Tommy Stevens. For a long time my mother thought there really was a boy by that name, the way I kept talking about him."

"Joey told the truth about seeing the ghost," Ted countered.

"That's so, he did, but that doesn't make up for all the times he *didn't* tell the truth. Know something? I'll bet if you were to ask him now if he saw the ghost, he wouldn't know for sure if he did or not. Let's face it, that kid simply doesn't know how to tell the truth, no matter how hard he tries. Someday I'd like to take him apart and see what makes him tick."

CHAPTER 15

An Explanation

Mr. Krillman was greatly relieved to find Joey with them, but he felt the boy deserved a little scolding.

"You shouldn't have gone off looking for Indians all by yourself, Joey. Besides, they live too far away. This summer we'll try to have an Indian or two come down to camp. Now I want you to promise me that you won't do it again."

"I won't," Joey pledged with great sincerity.

Then Mr. Krillman was told about the singing trees and the stranger, and he looked perplexed as he tried to figure out how much of it was true.

"I suppose," he remarked to Ted and Nelson as they walked over toward the mess hall, "that he really did wander off, and someone found him and showed him the way back. I didn't know that anyone was living in any of the cabins up that way, but it's quite possible. But as for the singing trees, I suppose Joey made that all up."

"I think he dreamed the whole thing," Nelson declared. "It sounds just like the sort of thing that somebody might dream—especially if he'd been thinking about it before."

"Did you ever dream about singing trees, my boy?" asked Ted.

"I did have one queer dream," Nelson retorted. "I dreamed I pinched myself to see if I was awake."

"That sounds kind of complicated," smiled Mr. Krillman. "Now let's see what we can rustle up in a hurry for lunch. These boys must be half-starved."

After lunch the young counselors renewed their task of repairing windows and made good progress, as Mr. Krillman kept the small boys occupied elsewhere. He promised to keep better track of them than he had that morning, when he had tried to attend to a little work at his desk while watching the boys play baseball outside his window. He had seen the boys running back and forth, but hadn't thought to count them, so that Joey had been gone more than an hour before he was missed.

"What about the ghost?" Nelson asked of Ted, as they took a little mid-afternoon breather. "Do you think he'll come back?"

Ted thought about it for several seconds. "No, I doubt he'll be back— ever again. But just on the chance he's got some new stunt planned for us, I think we ought to set up a little watch."

"All night?" asked Nelson with a yawn.

"No, just to midnight ought to be enough."

"Well, all right," Nelson agreed, "but if this ghost really has to get home by midnight, I'm going to call it Cinderella."

As he had promised, Ken Kutler returned that evening. He seemed anxious to talk alone with Ted, which came as something of a surprise to the latter. Since breaking his pact, Ted had expected that Ken would treat him a little distantly, but evidently Ken did not consider that their rivalry extended that far.

Of course Ted's eye immediately attracted attention, and explanations had to be made. Quickly Ted told his story. Ken had no questions to ask, but he had a decided grin as he listened, and Ted wondered what is considered so funny about a black eye. Then the reporter came around to business.

"Ted," Ken began, "I'm perfectly sincere with you in saying that the only story I am interested in here is the vandalism, but when we try to consider all the possible grounds for the vandalism, it often takes us far afield."

Ted wondered whether Ken was going to tell him what he knew about the mattresses and the missing money, but he soon found out that Ken was not going to take him into his confidence that far. Instead, Ken had another angle he was developing.

"Ted, I know we're supposed to be rivals, but you're just as anxious to discover what's back of this vandalism as I am. I'm frankly in it for a story, but as long as my interest and yours is the same in this matter, don't you think we might find it profitable to work together as much as we can?"

Ted nodded, a little skeptically, for Ken still wasn't talking about those mattresses.

Ken smiled. "All right, Ted, I admit that I'd try to beat you out on a story if I could, and I also admit I'm holding out something on you that I hope either to prove or disprove in a short while. Just now I want to talk about something else. One possible theory for the vandalism is that someone has some sort of commercial advantage to gain by driving the Y off the tract—probably, I would suppose, having to do with the development of lumbering on this tract. What would you say if you knew that someone had been carrying on such negotiations without the knowledge of Mr. Blair?"

"Why—I don't see how anybody could," said Ted uncertainly. "Mr. Blair's the director of the camp. He'd have to know about it."

"You'd think so, wouldn't you? But what if I could give you the name of this man? Then what do you think we should do about it?"

"Well, I—I suppose we ought to go to him and talk about it. I'm not condemning anybody unheard, and he ought to be given a chance to explain his position."

"All right, then, let's go and talk to Mr. Krillman. Now just a minute, Ted," he added quickly, as he saw Ted prepared to rush to the defense of his friend, "I'm not saying Mr. Krillman knows anything about the vandalism. I'm only saying that he's concealing one or two facts that might be of help to us. If you stop to think about it, there's no reason why he shouldn't. You're a junior counselor, and I'm an outside newspaper reporter, and he's not obliged to tell us anything. But if we knew what it was, we might be a step closer to the solution of this vandalism."

"You found out about Mr. Krillman stopping off in the woods, didn't you?" asked Ted shrewdly.

"Yes, and after doing a little further investigating of the matter, I found out who it was he was meeting. It's a man from the lumber company."

"A heavy-set man?" Ted questioned.

"Yes. You've seen him, then?" Ted nodded. "And of course the fact that Mr. Krillman chose to meet him out in the woods instead of here at camp suggests that perhaps Mr. Blair doesn't know anything about it."

He continued, as Ted seemed about to speak, "Never mind defending him, Ted. No doubt there is some perfectly good explanation which he will give us shortly. I want to tell you something else I discovered. I learned that this Y tract—whether the whole tract or merely one important segment of it, I'm not sure—originally belonged to Mr. Krillman's wife, and that she sold it to the Y."

"I don't see—" Ted began.

"Calm down, Ted. I'm not saying that Mr. Krillman has done anything wrong. Some people might say that because Mr. Krillman is a counselor here, his wife should have donated the land instead of selling it, but I believe that would be both unfair and unrealistic. If you were soliciting a donation to the Y from a person who wasn't at all wealthy— and Mr. Krillman isn't—and the person gave you ten or fifteen dollars, you'd think he was being very generous, wouldn't you? But it would be altogether too much to expect such a person to give you thousands of dollars. And yet that's what you'd be asking, if you expected him to donate valuable land."

"Then I don't understand what you're getting at," said Ted, puzzled.

"Only this. Since Mr. Krillman's wife once owned this land, he must know a great deal about the legal aspects, the commercial possibilities, and so on. And that's where I think we might be able to find a motive for the vandalism. That's why I think we ought to talk with Mr. Krillman."

He started toward the office. "Coming along?" he asked, as Ted hesitated.

"Oh, I guess so," Ted decided. He felt it would be embarrassing for him to question a man who was in fact his employer. On the other hand, he knew Mr. Krillman to be a devoted, conscientious camp leader, and was sure he hadn't done anything that couldn't be very readily explained. All Ted's newspaperman's instinct was to be in on anything that smelled of a story. And it was a story, wasn't it? Of course Mr. Krillman hadn't had anything to do with the vandalism or the "ghost. But if lumbering on the tract was being considered, then that certainly affected the trailerite story Carl Allison was working on.

Mr. Krillman was surprised to see them, and his welcoming smile faded a little as Ken came directly to the point.

"Mr. Krillman, I don t want to be impertinent, or to exceed the bounds of your hospitality, but some questions have come up, and I felt that you were the proper person to come to for answers. Is it true that you have been undertaking negotiations for lumbering on this tract?"

The counselor studied his face for a moment. "Yes, that's quite right," he, admitted.

"Isn't it also a fact that it was your wife who sold this tract to the Y?"

"I don't see any point in denying such a well-known fact," said Mr. Krillman quietly. "I might say that I had nothing to do with setting the price. That was done by an impartial committee, and a price agreed upon that was fair to all parties."

"I'd hate to see this land turned over to a lumber company, Ted remarked.

"Maybe you have the wrong idea about lumbering, Ted," Mr. Krillman explained. "Wood is a very important commodity in our economy. It gives us our newspapers and books, and most of our houses, as well as many other necessary things."

"And I suppose it gives men jobs," Ted added.

"Yes, Ted, and in this case perhaps more work than you realize. Due to our particular geography, lumbering in this entire section—not just on Y property—depends on whether or not the Y agrees to go along,"

"But isn't it also true," Ken went on, "that you were carrying on these negotiations without Mr. Blair's knowledge, and that was the reason you met the lumberman in the woods?"

"No, that is not true, or at least only partly true. Mr. Blair was fully aware of the possibility of our selling some of our trees, and gave me permission to go ahead in the matter, as long as I could make some arrangement which would not interfere with the camping season. There were two reasons why I arranged to meet Mr. Dryden away from camp, one being that I didn't care to have the boys passing around rumors of the lumbering before the matter had been settled. The other reason was that at the time I made the appointment I thought Mr. Blair would be here at camp, and I did not want him to know about the meeting. My reason for keeping it from him was that Mr. Dryden had told me a certain legal complication had come up. Since it was my wife who sold the property to the Y, you can understand that I was anxious over the possibility that some flaw had developed, that perhaps my wife's title to the property was not clear at the time she sold it. I hoped I could get the matter cleared up before Mr. Blair heard of it, since he has enough worries on his mind."

"Then did you learn the nature of the legal complication when you met Mr. Dryden?" Ken pursued.

"Yes, I did." Mr. Krillman frowned. "And I admit it's something that has disturbed me considerably. My wife's title to the property was perfectly legal, but in checking into the matter, the lumber company found that the northern and western boundaries to this tract are not completely clear. On my wife's deed the tract is identified simply by number, but in checking back further the company learned that the proper boundary dates all the way back to Homer Brintz and his so-called treaty or land purchase from the Indians. If any later survey was ever made, the records have been lost. As the legend states, the serpent rock was to mark the boundary between the land of the Indians to the north and the land of the white men to the south. Later the same serpent rock was used as a boundary between east and west—the Y tract and the farms—the rock forming the northwest corner of my wife's property. The proper western boundary of my wife's land was said to be 'a line drawn directly south from the serpent rock until it reaches the creek.' Now this poses a double predicament, for not only do we no longer know just where the serpent rock is located, but also the creek in the ravine has dried up, due to the fact that several farmers have sunk wells in the vicinity in recent years."

"Couldn't people who remember the creek swear out affidavits?" asked Ted.

"Well, perhaps, Ted, but I suppose to a lawyer a creek is a creek. Besides, we don't know exactly where the boundary line hit the creek, so that quite a number of acres of land are involved. At any rate, the lumber company informed me that they didn't feel they could go ahead with the proposition until the matter of the boundary was settled, since they wouldn't care to become involved in long legal proceedings." He continued musingly, "I never placed a great deal of stock in the old Indian legend, but it seems to me now if we could only find that treaty and the serpent rock, it might go a long way toward solving our problems."

"The treaty's probably destroyed by now," Ted opined. "Would it help if we found only the rock, but not the treaty?"

"Well, perhaps, Ted, but it might be difficult to prove this was the right rock. The treaty no doubt describes it more exactly."

Ken looked very much disappointed. "I can see that you do have a problem, Mr. Krillman. However, it doesn't appear to have any bearing on the matter of the vandalism."

"No, I don't see how it could. Surely the lumber company couldn't be responsible, for what would they have to gain? And I can't see how it would make much difference to anyone else whether we sell our trees, or fail to sell them."

But it did make a difference to some people, Ted thought, growing excited. Not only were there the other property owners who might hope to sell their trees, but there were all the men in the trailer camp, hoping to get work on the lumbering. But Ted did not openly mention the possibility—not with Ken Kutler there! This was getting too close to Carl Allison's trailer story.

"No, I surely can't see why a lumber company would set the woods on fire," Mr. Krillman mused.

"The fire!" Ken exclaimed, his brows tightening. Ted was so used to assuming that Ken knew everything that was going on that it came as a surprise to him that Ken had not associated the fire with the vandalism. He could almost see the reporter readjusting his thinking on the matter.

"And there's the 'ghost' to think about, too," Mr. Krillman went on. "Offhand, it looks like foolishness, but I must admit it's something I don't understand."

There seemed little more to say, and the conference came to an end soon afterward, with Ken thanking Mr. Krillman for talking to him.

CHAPTER 16

The Prowler

Ken and Ted left the office together and strolled back toward the line of cabins. It was a relief to Ted to see that Nelson had got the younger boys safely into bed, relieving him of the chore for the night. With the boys asleep or nearly asleep, Nelson came out to join Ted and Ken. Ken had already announced his intention of staying for the night, and was invited to join them in their cabin, but declined.

"If you don't mind, I think a cabin up on the other side of camp would not only be quieter, but would offer better possibilities for a visitation from the ghost," he said with a laugh.

"Ted and I are going to stay up watching until midnight," Nelson volunteered.

"You can watch if you want to," Ted contradicted, "but I'm tired, and I'm sure the ghost isn't going to come back tonight, anyway."

"You mean something we discovered today told you that?" asked Nelson, puzzled, for the last he had heard Ted was determined to stand guard.

"Yes," said Ted shortly.

They finally said good night, and Ted and Nelson left for their cabin.

"Only pretend to get undressed," Ted whispered, once they were inside the door.

"You mean we're going on guard? But you said"

"I said I was tired and I didn't think the ghost would be back tonight, but we're going to watch just the same."

"Until midnight?"

"Until morning if we have to," said Ted grimly.

"But why didn't you want Kutler and Mr. Krillman to know?"

"I don't want *anybody* to know. I think that's the reason we've been so unsuccessful so far. Too many people know what's going on."

They crept quietly out of the cabin. "We'll have to watch out for Argus," Ted reminded Nelson. "I think Mr. Krillman's got him tied up by his cabin, but he may notice us. If he does, be careful not to act at all sneaky, and then I don't think he'll bark at us."

"Well, where are we going to watch out for the ghost?" Nelson demanded.

"Hang the ghost! I told you already I don't think he'll be back."

"You mean you know who the ghost is? Then why don't you tell me?"

"Because you can figure it out just as easily as I can," said Ted impatiently, "just now I'm more interested in what Ken's up to."

"What do you think he's up to? He wouldn't steal anything, would he?"

"No, nothing—except a story, and that's the thing I've got to watch out for."

"Next you'll suspect *me* of something," Nelson grumbled.

"No danger," Ted grinned, "the way you hit the hay."

After an hour's slow wait it suddenly appeared that Ted's hunch was correct. The door of Ken's cabin slowly opened, and Ken stepped outside, looking to left and to right. Fortunately the boys were well concealed, and he did not spot them. Making sure that the coast was clear, Ken moved along briskly. He did not pass the boys' cabin, but he went behind the back of Mr. Krillman's cabin, boldly stopping to pat Argus on the head. The dog was well acquainted with him by this time, and gave him no trouble.

Then Ken moved on. To keep him in sight, the boys were also obliged to pass by Argus, and taking their cue from Ken, they also stopped to pat his head. Once again he did not bark, but he whined a little, coaxing to go along with them. They held their breaths for a moment, fearful lest Ken had taken alarm, but it seemed that he had not, for he did not look around.

Finally Ken stopped in front of the Hopi cabin. This was one of the cabins that had gone virtually undamaged, but Nelson recalled something about it.

"Say, Ted, there *was* a board pried loose on one of the windows. I'll bet the vandal *tried* to get in there but couldn't make it. Either it was too tough for him, or else he was interrupted."

They waited anxiously to see what Ken would do. It developed that it wasn't necessary for him to break in, for instead he drew a ring of keys from his pocket. After several attempts the door came open, and he went inside. There was a faint glow through the crack in the boards, and it seemed that he was using a flashlight, dimming it by holding his hand part way over the end.

Silently the boys crept up to the window and peered in. As Ted had already guessed, it was a mattress that engaged Ken's attention. He felt it all over carefully, but with just what results they could not say. Then they saw him extract a pocketknife from his pocket and switch open the blade.

"What'll we do now?" Nelson whispered.

"Let's go in. I hate this spying, and now that we've caught him in the act, I feel sure he'll tell us what this is all about."

They stepped up to the closed door and threw it open. Ken spun around, looking momentarily startled, and then his features relaxed.

"Well, Ted, I might have known I wasn't putting anything over on you. I suppose you want to know what I'm doing here, and I'm darned if I can think of anything you'll believe."

"How about the truth?" Nelson suggested.

"That might be just as hard to believe."

"Is this Mr. Raeburn's mattress?" Ted demanded.

The reporter's eyebrows rose. "Then you did catch on to that, didn't you? Ted, you're taking up right where your brother left off. What good did it do me to get rid of Ronald, when I've still got you on my tail?"

"Well?"

"Ted, I don't know. I've checked the mattresses back through the Y records, and I found that three mattresses had been donated to the Y from an itinerant secondhand dealer at about the time Mr. Raeburn's bed was sold. Apparently the dealer found that there were restrictions against carrying used mattresses for sale across his state line, and so he decided to give them away. I checked—"

They were interrupted just then by Argus's fierce barking.

"The ghost!" Nelson exclaimed. "Did he come back after all, just while we were tied up here?"

"Let's go and see!" Ted cried, but Ken stopped him.

"Don't bother. Argus is coming closer, and if I'm not mistaken, Mr. Krillman is with him. I don't think we're going to be bothered by the ghost tonight. *We're* the cause of the disturbance."

Presently Mr. Krillman stepped into the lighted doorway, the dog close at his heels.

"What's going on here?" he asked sternly. "Argus began whining, and I heard him and got up to see what was going on. Apparently something was."

"Well, I guess it would be rather long to explain," said Ken with an uneasy laugh.

"I've got all night. Ted, have you left the boys alone? I don't quite like that, in view of all the things that are going on around here."

"I'll go and check them," Ted replied, suddenly realizing that he and Nelson had been remiss. "Is it all right if I leave Argus on guard?"

"Do that," Mr. Krillman said shortly, still wondering about the meaning of this affair.

Ted hurried out, and found to his relief that the boys were all accounted for, and still asleep. Shutting Argus into the cabin with them, he hurried back. He found that during his absence Ken had explained a good deal of the story of the Raeburn mattress to Mr. Krillman. The counselor looked a little appeased but still not quite ready to forgive everything.

"Then it was you, Ken, who went into the office records yesterday?"

"Yes, Mr. Krillman, I did. I didn't feel that I was doing anything wrong, since there's nothing confidential there, and I knew you'd be glad to show me the records if I should ask."

"Then why didn't you ask?" Mr. Krillman questioned bluntly.

"For two reasons. The first was that I might be wrong, and I didn't want to appear as big a dope as I really am. The other"—he nodded toward Ted—"is that I have a rival here who gave me fair warning that he'd beat me to a story if he could, and he'd do it, too. So you see—"

"Is this Mr. Raeburn's mattress?" Ted interrupted, unable to contain himself any longer.

"I'm not sure, Ted. Through the office records I was able to locate the three mattresses which came from the dealer. That is, I was able to locate *two* of them. The third apparently has been discarded, and so I suppose there is little chance that we'll ever find it."

Nelson was busy feeling over the mattress with his hands. "I can't find anything in here," he decided.

"No, I couldn't either," Ken agreed. "However, we can't really tell for sure, unless we cut it open. Do I have your permission to do that, Mr. Krillman?"

"Oh, I suppose so, since you were going to cut it open *without* my permission ten minutes ago. And with so many mattresses ripped already, I suppose one more won't matter."

"If the money's in here, I'll personally see that you get a new mattress," Ken promised.

"And if it isn't, you'll personally sew this one up. Well, go ahead."

They waited expectantly as Ken sliced a series of three cuts, so that a large part of the cover of the mattress could be laid back, disclosing the cotton wadding beneath. There seemed to be no help for it; they would have to search through the cotton very carefully—for as Ken reminded them the money might be in the form of gold coins, hoarded from many years past, which would take up comparatively little space.

"Hold on!" Ted suggested. "No use making a mess of this mattress, until we check the other mattress. If it's the other one, we won't have to pull this one apart."

"And if it's this one, we won't have to pull the other one apart," Nelson opined, "so what've we got to lose either way?

"I mean, the money might be pretty bulky—gold's been out of circulation for a long time—and we might be able to find it from outside if it's in the other mattress."

They all agreed that this was pretty weighty logic for so late at night. In truth, the boys at least were beginning to feel a little slaphappy, for they had put in a long day.

"Which cabin has the other mattress?" asked Mr. Krillman.

"The Pueblo cabin, bed number five A," Ken informed them.

It happened that the Pueblo cabin was one in which the windows had been broken, although it had not been entered. They trekked over several trails until they reached it, and Mr. Krillman opened the door and switched on the light.

"That one," he said, indicating the bunk in the corner. "The A means upper, and just in case the mattresses have been switched, the number is sewed into the underside."

Ken hurried over to the bunk and felt along the surface of the mattress, investigating every lump, of which, unfortunately, there were quite a number. Not satisfied, he flung the mattress over and began feeling along the padding. He stopped suddenly, then pressed the same spot a number of times.

"Hear that?" he exclaimed, cocking an ear. They could all hear it now—a definite crinkling of paper.

"Well, this seems to be it," said Mr. Krillman, smiling for the first time that night.

"Unless the mattress just happens to be stuffed with paper," said Nelson jubilantly, but not believing it for a moment.

"I guess you won't object to my cutting this mattress, Mr. Krillman," said Ken deliberately to hide his own excitement. He took out his knife once more and carefully repeated the operation he had performed on the other mattress. They could easily hear the crinkling now—lots and lots of it. Maybe the mattress *had* almost been stuffed with paper, for $18,000 was a lot of paper, unless the bills were of very large denominations.

Then as Ken laid the surface of the mattress back they caught sight of tempting green stuff—money! Loads and loads of it! Money that had been secreted there many years ago by the eccentric Mr. Raeburn and had unexpectedly found its way to the Y camp, where so many queer things seemed to be happening all at once.

"Somebody's rich!" Nelson chanted.

"Who?" asked Ken suspiciously, and they noticed that all the elation had gone out of his voice.

"Why, the camp, I suppose, or maybe Mr. Raeburn's nephew"

"Wrong, Nelson, my boy, dead wrong. This is Confederate money, and not worth a dollar a bushel."

CHAPTER 17

At Serpent Rock

The group stared in silence at the pile of paper money, green, crinkled, and worthless. Well, perhaps not completely worthless, for it still retained a small souvenir value. During the Civil War its value had fluctuated with the tide of Confederate fortunes, and when defeat began to pile on defeat, and more and more money was printed, its value dwindled practically to nothing.

"Maybe Mr. Raeburn was a Southern sympathizer, and really thought the money was going to be worth something again," Nelson speculated.

"Not Mr. Raeburn," said Ken, shaking his head. "He was altogether too shrewd a man for that. No, this was his last big joke upon his nephew. He knew that if he told them he had the money, they would believe it, but he didn't promise them the money would be worth anything. And just to drag out the joke, he ordered the mattress sold to a traveling dealer. I suppose he really wanted his nephew to find it in the end, but in the meanwhile hoped he would endure months of expectation and disappointments and foolish searching before learning finally that there was no fortune waiting for him. Only maybe the nephew was smarter than I am, and gave up long ago, while *I* was the one who did the foolish running around, hoping I was going to get a story."

"You *did* get a story, didn't you?" Ted reminded him.

"A story? Oh, maybe a little one, not one tenth as good as it would have been if the money had turned out to be real. And it's a story that I almost hate to print, for it isn't going to portray me in a very flattering light."

"What about the couple who have been accused of stealing the money?" Ted inquired. "You can clear their reputation now, can't you?"

Ken brightened. "That's true enough. I'd forgotten about them. Well, I suppose there is some value in the story after all, although it won't be conclusive. People who thought they stole the money can just as easily suppose that they stole the real money and substituted the Confederate money. Funny, this couple were the ones who helped Mr. Raeburn when he was sick, and they were the ones whom he hurt the most. I suppose there's a lesson in that, but not a very good one."

"Won't it help a little that people will know now that Mr. Raeburn never had a fortune, and they can stop looking for it?" questioned Nelson.

"Oh, maybe, but since almost everybody has given up already anyway, my story won't change the situation very much. I'm afraid that so much time has passed that people have lost interest in Mr. Raeburn. Still, it is a story. I hope my editor will think it's worth a mattress or two before I blister my fingers patching these old ones up."

* * * *

As they walked slowly back toward their own cabins, Ken remarked to Ted, "Well, Ted, I guess I've been barking up the wrong tree. But I think this points up a very good reason why we ought to try to solve the mystery of this vandalism if we possibly can. As long as it is unsolved, suspicion shoots out in so many unexpected directions. The fact is, we don't seem to be any closer to discovering the vandal, and his motives for doing it, than we were the very first day. Who could it be? A group of disgruntled Indians? Highly improbable. The lumber company? I don't see how it would help them any. Someone from the trailer camp? The trailerites weren't even out here at the time of the fire last fall. Other timber owners around here? I'm sure they understand the Y wouldn't stand in their way if they wanted to sell their trees. Mr. Krillman explained satisfactorily the presence of the lumberman in the woods. And I'm sure now it wasn't the Raeburn heirs—I saw a glaring weak point in that when I learned about the fire, for why should they want to burn the camp down? Then who's left?"

Ted shook his head.

"Did you see the *Town Crier* today, Ted?" Ted had not. "There was a real fighting editorial on the front page on behalf of the trailerites. I recall one line of it: 'Our children belong in schools, while their elders are quarreling over tax problems.' Everybody pays attention when Mr. Dobson gets riled up. I wouldn't be surprised if he got some action."

Ken continued—Nelson and Mr. Krillman were out of earshot, walking more slowly behind: "I'm not interested in Carl Allison's trailerite story, Ted. As a matter of fact, I wouldn't dare to be, since a newspaper stays pretty clear of a rival's crusade. As long as I was following up a lead without telling you about it, I don't blame you for breaking our friendship treaty. But the way things stand, why don't we become friends again?"

"All right, Ken, we're friends again, but only on the vandalism story. Now what have you got to tell me?"

Ken laughed. "So you wanted to be sure I didn't come into the partnership empty-handed? I'm afraid that's the case, though, Ted. I don't have an inkling about this vandalism."

"Do you think now it was the work of juvenile delinquents?"

"No, I don't, Ted," said Ken seriously. "Oh, it could have been done by a young person, even a teenager, but not the kind we ordinarily think of as juvenile delinquents—irresponsible kids without enough to do. This was serious and full of desperation or hate. I can't figure out what the motive was, but there is some deep, bitter motive, of that I'm sure." He waited a moment. "All right, Ted, do you have anything to tell *me?*"

"I'm not sure," said Ted thoughtfully. "Actually, I've got only one clue to go on, and I'm not even sure it's a real clue. It's a man staying up in a cabin in the hills." And he proceeded to tell Ken about Joey's story.

Ken considered the story carefully. "It's hard to say, Ted. The whole thing could be simply Joey's imagination, or it could be true enough but not important to our present purpose. Or it could turn out to be something very significant. At least it's worth checking on."

The group came to a parting of the ways, and said good night, Ted telling Mr. Krillman they would keep Argus with them the rest of the night. The two boys chatted awhile in a low voice as they undressed, running over the new development, but both were very tired and glad to fall into bed.

They saw little of Ken in the morning, for he left before breakfast. He was already in his car as they came out of their cabin, and he called to them:

"Don't let that blizzard freeze you out."

"Is there really a blizzard on its way?" asked Ted. He could well believe it, for the skies were gray, and a cold wind made him shiver a little in his light sweater.

"That's what the weatherman says—sometime tomorrow—and he's occasionally right." With a wave of the hand he drove off.

At breakfast Mr. Krillman brought up the subject of the blizzard. By unanimous consent, it was decided to finish out the week at camp anyway. Ted was sent to town to call the boys' mothers and pick up some warmer clothes for them, while Nelson took the younger ones on a promised hike.

The hikers were ready to leave soon afterward. A little lunch was taken along, although they expected to be back by noon, or not long after.

"Why don't you try to find the Valley of the Singing Trees?" Ted suggested. "Maybe Joey can show you the way."

"Well, maybe," Nelson agreed, rather doubtfully. "If there is such a place. Mr. Krillman didn't seem to take much stock in Joey's story when he heard it. But I don't have anywhere else in mind, so I suppose we could look for that as easily as anything."

They set off in high spirits, Argus rambling along happily. The boys appeared not to care very much in which direction they went, just as long as they were going somewhere.

"Joey, which way did you go, when you went looking for Indians yesterday?"

"I guess it was this way," Joey answered, nodding toward the north, but he didn't seem very sure about it. Privately, Nelson wondered whether it could be so. The area to the north was more hilly and heavier wooded, while to the south the land gradually leveled out into a broad river valley. Quite possibly Joey had intended to go northward, where he had been told there were Indians living in the hills, and it would have been easier for him to become lost there. On the other hand, Mr. Krillman and the other boys had failed to find him there, though somehow he had found his own way home. Maybe he hadn't come north at all.

The hiking party first skirted the borders of Lake Pioneer, then headed up along the small stream that fed the lake. This stream, in turn, was fed by numerous other smaller streams or brooks, a few so large it was difficult to determine which was the main stream and which was the branch. In some cases boards had been laid across to make a rude bridge; in others they were forced to cross on rocks, but were lucky enough to experience only an occasional wet foot. Besides these, numerous "dry" small valleys or ravines emptied out into the various streams. Perhaps they had at one time carried water, or perhaps they still did so in the wetter seasons, but now they were quite dry.

The whole northern tract, then, consisted of a meshwork of valleys, which led in turn to other valleys (much like a picture of human veins in his hygiene book, Nelson thought), while the hills between became ever larger and more rugged. This was a wild tract, and Nelson wondered if it had ever been fully explored or mapped. At least much of it seemed very strange to him, though he had taken many hikes there when he was a little younger. Of course there was very little danger that adults or older boys would become lost, for if they did, all that was necessary was to head downstream, which would have led them to the main stream and inevitably to Lake Pioneer, just as the branches of a folding fan all lead to the main stem. But younger boys might not be aware of this simple device and could easily become confused and frightened.

From time to time Nelson asked Joey, "Is this the way you came?" to which Joey replied uncertainly, "I guess so." He seemed very hazy about it all, and no wonder, Nelson thought, for he more than half-suspected Joey was trying to lead them through his dream.

"There was sunshine yesterday," Joey explained, as though this made a great difference. And possibly it did to him, Nelson thought. A heavy overcast would change the color of everything, and to a small boy shapes would seem more varied, distances different.

Although Joey was not aware of it, he was in fact the leader of the party, for Nelson was following his directions just as well as he could. Finally, Joey led them off the main stream and up one of the tributaries. Half a mile farther on he hesitated.

"I think it's this way," he decided, indicating a short dry-bed ravine.

And now Nelson felt certain that Joey was hopelessly confused. This surely couldn't be the Valley of the Singing Trees, for there were very few trees here. The ravine was merely a short, dead-end abutment, which would have attracted few hikers because it led nowhere. Whether many had ever come here was difficult to determine, for there was no path. It was hardly necessary, for the ground was now rocky and barren of vegetation, and the party did not remain in single file, as they were often forced to do in following the previous streams.

Well, what did they have to lose, Nelson thought. With Joey lost in his reckoning, they had no hope of finding the Valley of the Singing Trees that day. They might as well explore this little valley, as long as Joey wanted them to, since it was still too early to turn back.

They headed up the valley, the boys scrambling wildly about and stopping to pick up and examine odd-shaped or unusual-colored rocks. Many of these went into their pockets. Only as they approached the end of the valley did Nelson begin to suspect that something was wrong. This wasn't a dead-end valley after all, for there was a turn, not apparent from the valley's mouth. And when they made the turn, his jaw fell open in wonder, for before them lay a beautiful valley, with lush bushes and tall trees, all the more beautiful because its presence was unsuspected.

Could this be the famous Valley of the Singing Trees? It was wonderful, unusual, and secret enough to have a legend grow up about it. Only one thing was missing: the trees weren't singing. Nelson felt a rising excitement. Joey couldn't be wrong now, for he had led them here all by himself. Still Nelson told himself to be careful. The discovery of the valley could have been accidental, and even if it wasn't, Joey could still have imagined the part about the singing trees.

"What's that strange pile of rocks?" asked one of the boys, pointing with his finger.

It was indeed unusual. As they came closer, Nelson saw it wasn't a pile of rocks, but rather one rock, worn into its queer, twisted shape by the action of wind and rain.

The serpent rock! For the first time Nelson recalled this portion of the legend. If this was really the Valley of the Singing Trees, and this was the famous serpent rock, then the treaty might be buried under it!

He hurried the boys along until they reached the base of the rock. Then he saw they were too late. If the treaty had ever been buried there, they weren't going to find it, for somebody had been digging there recently.

CHAPTER 18

Allison Speaks His Mind

Ted drove into Forestdale, intending to stop off briefly at home, but decided to stop at a drugstore to make his calls instead. As long as they were long-distance calls, he preferred to pay for them himself, rather than have them added to the monthly phone bill.

All the mothers had bundles of warmer clothing they wanted him to pick up, and Ted did so. Then suddenly he felt a longing to talk over the whole mystery with his brother Ronald. He couldn't do a lot of explaining over the long-distance telephone, but he remembered that Ronald would have received his *Town Crier* by today and so would already know a lot of the details.

Ted put through a person-to-person call to Ronald at the newspaper office, then waited for the operator to complete it. The switchboard girl at the newspaper answered, and plugged in to Ronald's phone, but it wasn't Ronald's voice that came on the wire next.

"I'm sorry, but Mr. Wilford didn't come in today. No, I don't know of any way he can be reached by phone. I understand he's out of the city."

The operator asked Ted whether he would care to speak with anyone else, but he said no, thanked her, and hung up, disappointed.

With the coming of a blizzard, this would probably be Ted's last chance to get his sports story in to the *Town Crier,* and he stopped off at home for it. To his surprise, he found the door unlocked, although his mother didn't appear to be anywhere around on the ground floor. He went upstairs, and was about to pass Ronald's old room when he stopped suddenly. Ronald was asleep on the bed!

"Ron!" he cried.

Aroused, Ronald sat up sleepily but good-humoredly. "Well, Ted, is that you?" He opened his eyes very wide in surprise. "Or is it you? I've got a feeling one of us isn't seeing very well. Which door did you walk into?"

"Never mind about that. What are you doing home?"

Ronald stretched. "Oh, I've been putting in a good deal of overtime lately, tracking down a story, and the boss thought I was entitled to a few days' rest. I'll tell you all about it when we've got more time." He nodded toward a copy of the *Town Crier* lying on the table. "It looks like you've been having lots of excitement around here."

"Enough," and Ted gave him a rather brief sketch of everything that had been happening.

"Any theories?" asked Ronald, looking not so sleepy now.

"Just that the man in the cabin might have something to do with it. And these." Ted drew the rock samples from his pocket.

Ronald picked them up and examined them carefully. "I'm afraid I don't know enough about it to say, but it surely wouldn't do any harm to get these samples analyzed. Did you find these on Y property?"

"No, on Mr. Thompkins' farm, just the other side of the ravine."

"Do you want me to take care of it for you, Ted?"

"If you don't mind, I'm due back at camp soon. But say," he added, "I don't care much about going there while you're home."

"Oh, don't mind me, Ted. After driving all night it'll be hours before I'm good for anything. Besides, I'll have things to do. There's this errand, and I'll want to stop in and see Mr. Dobson, and—"

"And Ken?"

"Yes, Ken, but I don't dare bother him until his Thursday-noon deadline is past. Probably we'll have lunch together tomorrow, and then I may drive down to camp later."

"Ron," said Ted seriously, "do you think I'm doing the right thing working along with Ken on this vandalism story?"

Ronald smiled. "I think you sometimes take yourself too seriously, Ted. Of course you do work for the *Town Crier,* on a limited basis, but you seem to be forgetting that you also work for Mr. Krillman. It's important to him to get this vandalism cleared up, and as long as Ken's working on the story, it seems to me you have an obligation to help him out if you can."

Ted immediately felt better about it. "Just the same," he insisted, "I'm going to feel pretty silly about it if Ken pulls off a big story right under my nose."

Ted's school sports story for the *Town Crier* still had to be typed, and he got out his portable and went to it, while Ronald made some very unhelpful comments. Reluctantly, Ted took his leave.

He no longer felt quite comfortable at the newspaper office now that Carl Allison had established himself solidly in Ronald's old position. Allison had three confirmed antagonisms: toward Ronald, Ted, and Ken Kutler. Ted wasn't quite able to trace the first of these, but suspected that in his last few days on the paper Ronald had been overzealous about showing his successor the ropes. Some of Allison's feeling toward Ronald must have rubbed off on Ted, while in Ken Kutler Allison saw only a dangerous rival. Allison seemed to get along well enough in his relations with Mr. Dobson, Miss Monroe, and the people he had to meet as a reporter.

This time Ted's luck was bad, for Miss Monroe was out and Allison was in, and in a particularly belligerent mood. Allison was a tall young man, good-looking enough except when he was scowling as he was now.

"You're just the one I wanted to see, Wilford," he said at once.

"Did you?" asked Ted casually, knowing that it wasn't about anything good.

"Yes. You must think you're pretty hot stuff, don't you, correcting my story? So the vandal entered four cabins instead of three, and I said there were fifty windows broken instead of fifty-seven. What difference does that make to our readers?"

"We might as well get it as accurate as we can," said Ted evenly. Although Allison was angry, Ted didn't think this was the real thing he was angry about.

"The way I understood the setup," Allison went on, "you were to be the high-school correspondent and I was the regular reporter. You were to cover anything at school, and I was to cover the rest of the town, and we were going to stay out of each other's hair."

"Isn't that how it is?" asked Ted coolly.

"No. Oh, I know how you've been making up to Mr. Dobson, trying to get my job away from me after you graduate." Ted was amazed. He had never given any thought to working full time on the Town *Crier.* After graduation he was faced with four years of college and a possible military hitch, and by that time almost anything could happen.

"You're dreaming," was about all he could say.

"I'm dreaming, am I? Look how you got that story of the safe robbery at school away from me last fall." This was hardly the truth of the matter. The story had come to Ted almost by default, because Allison, in Mr. Dobson's absence, refused to work overtime. Ted began to get mad.

"I didn't mind so much about that," Allison proceeded, "because that happened at school. But I might have had a scoop at the trial, if you hadn't been palling around with Ken Kutler—" Once more his facts were wrong, for Ted was sure the money would never have been recovered if it hadn't been for Ken.

"Ken's all right," Ted broke in angrily.

"Maybe, but you seem to forget that he works for a rival paper and would swipe his grandmother's false teeth for a story."

"All right, so I'm friendly with Ken," Ted retorted. "As long as I'm only the high-school correspondent, and not concerned about anything else, I don't see what I can possibly tell Ken that will do him any good. As for being correspondent, I'd resign this minute and never come near the office, except that I've too much respect for Mr. Dobson."

"You make things *sound* all right, Wilford, but somehow they don't turn out that way. What were you doing hanging around the trailer camp the other morning?" he demanded.

So that was it! Allison was afraid Ted was cutting in on his story about the trailerite situation, and that was the reason for his bitterness. Ted was glad to understand but still amazed.

"This was part of the reason," he said, opening his injured eye wide with his fingers.

"I suppose you got that eye sticking it somewhere it didn't belong. Well, just make sure you don't stick your nose where it doesn't belong hereafter."

"Nuts!" Ted retorted, and was about to tell Allison to mind his own business when Miss Monroe's arrival put an end to the discussion.

CHAPTER 19

The Return of Argus

"Has Argus come back yet?"

This was the hail from the young hikers as they approached camp and saw Ted outside, working with Mr. Krillman. To save the strain on his voice, Ted waited till they were a little closer before replying.

"No, wasn't he with you?"

By this time Nelson was close enough to answer in a nearly normal voice. "He was for a while. Then he saw a chipmunk or something and ran off. We whistled for him and he didn't come, and then we started for home. We thought he'd soon catch up with us, but he didn't."

"He'll be back by dark," Mr. Krillman prophesied. "He likes to ramble alone out in the woods. But he also likes a hot evening meal and a warm bed by the fire."

Ted was glad to lay off work for a while and talk, for he wasn't feeling very cheerful. He missed Ronald, and his run-in with Allison had left him with a slow burn.

"Did you find the singing trees?" he asked of Nelson, as Mr. Krillman went off to round up the boys and get them ready for lunch.

"I still don't know, Ted," Nelson answered thoughtfully. "Joey did lead us to a strange valley, and there was a rock that looked very much like a coiled serpent, and someone had been digging around it, but we didn't hear any singing trees."

After lunch Ted and Nelson set to work on the windows once more, getting a good deal done, so that by evening the most exposed windows had all been replaced. Fortunately for the junior counselors, Mr. Krillman saw to it that the younger boys left the workers alone, or else very little would have been accomplished.

Following supper even Mr. Krillman was beginning to grow worried, for Argus had not yet returned. Before bedtime, everyone went outside and whistled for him, and even took a short walk from camp in search for him, but to no avail. Finally Mr. Krillman would let them look no longer, and herded them off to bed.

"Blizzard tomorrow," Ted yawned as the young counselors began to follow the example of the smaller campers.

"If the weatherman doesn't change his mind by morning," Nelson returned. "That's the way it usually happens."

But this time the weatherman, far from changing his mind, only confirmed his opinion and re-enforced it with more definite facts. The cold front would arrive, he said, about four o'clock in the afternoon, accompanied by rising winds and at least six inches of snow. It was all hard to believe, for in the morning, though it was cool, the sky was still bright and unclouded.

While they were sitting at the breakfast table there was a scratching at the door, and when it was opened Argus came prancing in. He leaped about and nosed up to everyone, but seemed to keep a little eye out for Mr. Krillman, too, as though aware he had done something he shouldn't. But the counselor was too glad to see him to scold him, and looked visibly relieved as he stooped to pat the dog's head. Everyone else was happy about the return of their friend, too, though the younger boys showed it the most.

"He doesn't look very hungry," Ted observed, as the dog smelled and then refused a small tidbit one of the boys offered to him.

"No, and it doesn't look to me like he's spent the night out in the open," said Mr. Krillman. "He had shelter of some sort."

"And we know it wasn't Woody Preston that fed him," Nelson pointed out, "because he's allergic to dogs."

"The dog's lost his collar somewhere, too. He was wearing it yesterday when he left."

Having decided to break up camp on Saturday, weather permitting, Mr. Krillman drove off to talk to an elderly man he had mentioned before, for he felt they should no longer allow the camp to be unguarded. Nelson was assigned to various jobs for which his carpentry skill particularly suited him, while this time Ted was placed in charge of the small boys.

Following lunch, Mr. Krillman had to leave again. He had decided it was wise to stock up on plenty of supplies, perhaps much more than they would actually need, in view of the uncertain weather. As long as he had made arrangements for a watchman, he didn't mind leaving their surplus stock at camp to wait till summer. Unfortunately, he hadn't been able to get the supplies he wanted in sufficient quantity that morning, and would have to go back for them, and because some of the boxes would be pretty heavy, he decided that Ted should go along with him.

Nelson directed the boys in an exciting game of touch football which, piled on top of their morning exercise, took a good deal of the starch out of them. Afterward they had warm chocolate milk and cookies. Then, noticing they were rather tired, Nelson, with tongue in cheek, suggested a nap. The suggestion was greeted with incredulous protests, until he told them that if they did sleep, he would persuade Mr. Krillman to let them stay up a little longer that night.

With the boys settled down, Nelson thought he should finish up a few odd jobs—"battening down the hatches," as he expressed it—before the coming of the storm.

"Everybody go to sleep—and Joey," he warned, "no wandering off in search of Indians," though afterward he was to blame himself for having put the idea in Joey's mind.

"I won't," Joey promised.

Ted's and Mr. Krillman's marketing mission was filled with frustrating delays, but they were finished at last and headed back toward camp. Snowflakes were already drifting down, a prelude to the greater storm they knew was coming. They stopped at the Metlow farm for Mr. Krillman to make a telephone call, and he came out looking worried.

"Ted, I've called the office, and a few things have come up that I think I'd better attend to right away, before the snowstorm. You can take the car and go back to camp. I'll ride into town with Mr. Metlow."

"How will you get back?"

"I'll drive down with Mr. Blair, who is returning to camp this evening. We'll be back before the storm cuts us off."

Ted drove on to camp, where he was greeted by Nelson, and the two of them went off together to see about arousing the boys. It was then they made the discovery that Joey's bed was empty.

"What's happened to Joey?" Nelson demanded of the others.

"He went to get a drink," he was told.

"A drink! Didn't you kids have all the milk you wanted before you lay down? When did he go?"

"Just before we went to sleep."

"That makes it at least an hour ago," Nelson groaned. "What was he wearing?"

"He put on his jacket and his cap, and everything," he was informed. "We told him he didn't need a jacket just to get a drink, but he said it was going to snow."

"That kid," said Nelson, shaking his head despairingly. "I might have known a promise didn't mean anything to him. I should never have taken my eyes off him for a minute. Where do you suppose he's gone?"

"To the Valley of the Singing Trees, of course," said Ted with quick intuition, "and that's where I'm headed right now."

"Why you? If anybody goes, I'm the one to do it. I know the way—"

"And that's exactly the reason I'm going. It's more important that you should be available to lead the rescue party. Better bundle these kids up in the car and take them to the Metlow farm, where you can call the police. Maybe I'll be able to find Joey myself, but with this storm picking up we don't dare take a chance. Is Argus with him?"

"He must be. I don't see him anywhere around." He gave Ted as explicit directions as he could for finding the valley, then added, "Hadn't you better take something along with you, Ted?"

Ted had matches and a pocket flash, but he decided not to take anything else. He wanted to travel light, and with any further delay might miss his chance of finding Joey before dark. In a few minutes he was off.

Although Ted did not know it then, he was actually not very far behind Joey, and might have had little difficulty overtaking him had he been certain of himself. Instead, he felt obliged to go carefully and take his bearings from time to time—although he wondered if it was any use, for if he was having this much trouble keeping to the trail, it was quite possible that Joey had lost the trail long before. Actually, Ted really made very little better time than Joey.

On and on he marched, the snow clinging heavily to him. Ted had no fears for himself. The wind and moist snow held no danger for him, unless he should suffer an unexpected accident. If necessary, he could walk all night, and easily find his way out of the woods in the morning. The wetness of the snow told him that the temperature was barely below freezing—but that was too cold for Joey, alone and lost in the wooded hills, with little knowledge of how to protect himself.

Then Ted was lucky enough to come across what looked like a footprint, only partly blown over, though how long ago it had been made he could not guess. He scanned the trail ahead as far as he could see, but Joey was nowhere in sight. His impulse was to plunge recklessly ahead, but he controlled himself. It wouldn't do to go ahead too fast, and perhaps lose himself and these precious clues which meant so much. So he moved ahead cautiously, and was gratified when he managed to pick up another footprint in a sheltered spot. He had traveled for a mile and more, making so many turns that he lost track of them, before he felt convinced he was gaining on Joey. He called from time to time, but his voice was lost in the wind, and there was no answer. On and on he plunged, up and down hill, across creeks, and through thick woods, still calling whenever he thought there was any hope at all.

It was Argus who saved the day. At a critical moment, when Ted hadn't found any footprints for some time, he heard a bark off to the side, in a slightly different direction from that which he had been following.

Without that bark, he would surely have passed the wanderers by in the dark, and might never have picked up their trail again.

Striking off toward the sound of the dog, he discovered Joey, exhausted, leaning up against a tree. Argus was sitting beside him, and apparently it was the fact that Joey had stopped which encouraged Argus to bark.

Joey could hardly have been more glad to see him, although he did not act at all surprised.

"I knew you'd find me, Ted," he said simply, with a great deal more confidence than Ted himself had felt.

"But Joey, didn't you promise not to go looking for Indians?"

"I wasn't looking for Indians," he explained. "I was looking for the singing trees."

This was no time to scold the boy, but if Joey had any notion where they were, which was more than Ted did, now was the time for him to speak up.

"Where are we now, Joey? Do you have any idea?"

"I don't know," Joey answered, beginning to sniffle.

"All right, don't cry. You're all right now."

But Ted knew they were far from all right. It was already pitch dark, and he saw little chance of their getting back to camp before morning. "Go downhill" was a good motto on a clear day, but on a stormy night it was nearly worthless. Finding the trail back to camp would involve a long process of trial and error, and Ted knew Joey would be exhausted long before that. Besides, he had only a small flashlight, which he didn't dare turn on very often for fear it would burn out, and he knew that the trail led dangerously close to the stream in places. In the dark they might easily fall into the water and risk pneumonia.

If only he knew where they were... If he did, he could judge the possibility of finding some shelter, or of contacting the rescue party which he was certain was on the way. But not knowing, the best thing he could do was build a fire and try to construct the best shelter he could with the aid of his pocketknife.

Then he became aware of a low murmur which seemed to fill the air about him. It was a melody, and yet not like any other melody he had ever heard before. It rose and fell, and came and went, seemingly without pattern or design. It was so soft and distant he thought it was fading away altogether, and yet it remained sharp and distinct. Where did it come from? They were in a sheltered valley, and not conscious of the blowing wind, and yet it was all around them, everywhere, like New Year's bells, tangible but untraceable, surely one of the most unusual and most moving experiences of his life.

"It's the singing trees!" Joey exclaimed happily. "Now I know where we are."

"Well, I'll be darned!" said the flabbergasted Ted, in a soft tone in keeping with the melody all around them.

CHAPTER 20

The Man in the Cabin

After having called the police, Nelson sat in Mr. Metlow's living room and fumed. He wanted to be off on the search himself, as Ted was, but the police had told him to wait until they got there. The four small boys hung around him in a group, all very solemn. Then the first police car arrived, and Nelson told his story in careful detail.

"Can't we get off and start looking for them?" he asked impatiently, as the officer showed no signs of moving.

"Just keep your shirt on for a few minutes," said the officer in charge. "The more haste the less speed. We've got a rescue truck on the way, and it'll have all the equipment and supplies we need. Then we can organize a proper search. If we go shooting off in all directions, there's almost certain to be an accident to someone, and the chances are it won't be to Joey."

Ronald and Ken were the next to arrive, in Ken's car. Ken had heard the police report over the shortwave radio and immediately gotten in touch with Ronald. Ted's brother was looking very thoughtful. Although he knew the danger to Ted was much less than to Joey, it brought the matter closer to home.

Other cars began to arrive. Mr. Krillman came in Mr. Blair's car, and some of the neighbors began to come in. With each new group, Nelson had to tell his story over again, although he really had very little to tell.

Although Mr. Krillman was looking very worried, he found one ray of hope. "Are you sure Argus was with him?" he asked Nelson.

"Oh, yes. That's how we knew for sure he was gone, and not just hanging around camp."

"Well, then, he'll come out of it all right. As long as Argus is with him, nothing's going to happen to him." He spoke more hopefully than he really felt.

A second patrol car arrived, bringing an unexpected newcomer in the person of Woody Preston.

"We found him hanging around," the officer explained, "and since his car matches the description of one we've been told to watch out for, we brought him in."

"You did not!" Woody contradicted. "I came because I wanted to. I heard about the accident over my car radio, and I thought maybe I could help."

"Let's put it this way," said the officer grimly. "He came because he wanted to, but if he hadn't wanted to, he would have come just the same."

Ronald nodded toward Woody as he asked Ken:

"Is this the boy you were telling me about, the one who's been play-ing the ghost around camp?"

"He's the one, all right," Ken affirmed. "It was just his notion of some monkey business, I guess. As far as I can tell he didn't do any real harm except to give the campers a lively week. I thought right from the first the ghost affair didn't have anything to do with the vandalism. The real vandal wouldn't risk hanging around like that, when he knew everybody was looking for him. Finally, Ted caught Woody at some of his monkeyshines, and that was the end of the ghost at camp."

Probably no one was as much surprised at this revelation as Nelson, although he tried to conceal it.

Then Woody *had* done it all! But how had he managed to get away with so many things without getting caught? Nelson looked at Woody, almost with a feeling of awe.

Ronald also turned to Woody. "Didn't you have anything better to do than act like a kid?"

"Not very much," Woody admitted. "That wasn't my big reason, though. I thought maybe I could get things stirred up a little, so there'd be something in the newspapers, and people would start to think about the people in the trailer camp and how they couldn't get work because the lumbering didn't go through. The papers didn't print anything about the ghost, but they did do something for us trailer campers. We just got a notice that the school board changed its mind and was readmitting all the trailer children to school."

"Looks like Mr. Dobson's campaign is paying off," Ken remarked.

"It usually does," said Ronald with satisfaction.

"I guess Ted knew all along it was you, Woody," Nelson recollected. "Anyway, he did after we found the stilts. He knew then it was a kid's stunt. But I still can't figure out how you did everything. How did you get that big siren into camp all by yourself?"

"Oh, it wasn't too hard, with ropes and things! I did it before you came to camp. That's why I needed my car. Most of the time I used that secret path I'd found, but that wouldn't do for the heavy siren. And if I was going to drive out there, I figured I'd better not do it at night, for somebody would sure know something was wrong if they heard me. So I drove out right in the open daylight, and hoped nobody would notice me. Maybe Mr. Metlow saw me, but not close enough to tell who I was. I saw the damage to the camp, but I decided not to let that stop me. It fitted in with what I was trying to do."

"How did you get into and out of camp so many times?" asked Nelson, puzzled.

"When do you mean?"

"Well, Sunday night. You must have made about four trips into camp."

Woody was enjoying his little joke. "What makes you think I was there four times? Do you know how many times I was really there? Not once!"

"But you must have been, unless it was somebody else," Nelson persisted. "How did you set the siren?"

"Oh, I set that Saturday night, the same night I ran through the camp on stilts wearing that sheet that I'd treated with luminous paint. I tried to make enough noise so somebody'd be sure to see me, and I guess I did, for I got the dog barking."

"Weren't you afraid somebody might take a shot at you?" asked Ken.

"No. Who's to do it? Nelson and Ted wouldn't have guns, and everybody knows Mr. Krillman won't touch a gun ever since the war."

"What about Mr. Blair?"

"Was he there? I didn't know that. If I had, I guess I would have been more careful." His laugh was not quite so easy now.

"But even if you didn't set the siren Sunday night," Nelson continued, "you still must have made three trips into camp: one to break the string so the siren would go off, another time to paint the warning sign on the wall, and still another time to erase the sign."

"No, I didn't have to break the string. I had it treated with some acid that would slowly eat through the string and break it. I'd experimented with it until I was pretty sure it would go off during the night. And I didn't paint the sign Sunday night. I did that Saturday night, when I figured you wouldn't be watching so carefully because I hadn't started my tricks yet. You didn't see the sign on Sunday because it wouldn't show in daylight. And I didn't go back to erase the sign. The rain must have taken care of that for me. This luminous paint I used wasn't like ordinary paint that sticks to the wood and hardens. The rain would have washed it off."

"Were you trying to make us think the Indians did it? Is that why you painted the scroll, and dropped the feathers?"

"Well, I wasn't exactly trying to blame it on anybody else, but I thought it made an interesting touch."

"It looks like you put in a pretty busy week," Ronald commented. "What were you doing Friday night?"

"I went to a movie that night. There was a good picture showing—all about ghosts. I thought I'd pick up some new ideas, but I didn't. I did have a plan for hooking my record player up to a loud-speaker and making it sound like the trees were singing, but I couldn't work it out."

As the search was organized, a difficult decision faced Mr. Krillman. "Do you want to concentrate on the north side of camp," the officer asked, "or should we spread out in all directions?"

They didn't like to divide their forces, and the north side was certainly the most likely. To the west was the ravine and ridge, between which the camp road wound, and behind this lay the farms. It didn't seem probable that Joey had gone that way. The east was cut off by the lake and stream. But how could they be sure Joey hadn't gone south? Knowing how unpredictable—and how lost—a small boy can be, Mr. Krillman felt that he couldn't take a chance.

"Let's concentrate on the north, but we'd better send a couple of men south, just in case."

By the time the rescue truck arrived, the house was full of people milling around. Nelson wondered if Mr. Thompkins, Mr. Metlow's disagreeable neighbor, would show up, but he did not put in an appearance. Later Nelson heard someone remark that Mr. Thompkins had been away from his farm all day.

The police force showed its competence in making the plans for the search. The rescue truck had brought them everything they would need: tents, plenty of lanterns, a couple of portable stoves, food, and provisions for warm drinks, blankets, first-aid supplies, and a mobile unit for keeping in touch with the camp. In a few minutes the large party was ready to take off: the officers, the counselors, the two reporters, Woody, Nelson, Mr. Metlow, and the neighbors who had volunteered to join the search.

Upon reaching camp—and finding that Ted had not returned—two officers were dispatched southward, another stayed there on duty at the radio, while all the others headed northward, following the plan that had already been drawn up, with Nelson, who had visited the valley before, showing the way as best he could. The searchers were spread out on a wide front, but within communicating distance of each other. It was slow, painstaking work in the blinding snow, for they wanted to be as careful and as thorough as they could.

Some two hours later, when it was well after dark, the officer in charge decided to call a temporary halt. He wanted to collect any stragglers and make sure no one was missing from their party. A tent was set up and arrangements made for some hot refreshments.

"I don't want to sound gloomy," said the officer in a low voice to the little group around him, "but this snow is getting awfully deep. I'm afraid we're at the stage already where it would be difficult for a little boy to walk."

"Maybe Ted's found him and could carry him for a while," Nelson suggested.

"Well, we'll hope so, but they couldn't make much progress that way in the dark and with the uncertain footing. Our best hope is that they've found some sort of shelter. How close do you think we are to that valley now?"

Nelson could only shake his head. "We ought to be pretty close, but it's hard for me to tell in the storm this way. Anyway, we don't know for sure that Joey or Ted ever reached the valley."

"Aren't there some cabins around here?" Ronald questioned.

"I didn't see any when I was here before, but there must be. Joey said he saw a man, and the man must have been staying at a cabin."

"He probably was," Mr. Krillman agreed, "for that would fit in with the way Argus was gone overnight. Well, let's not stand here much longer," he addressed the officer.

The officer was about to reply, when his partner came up to report.

"There's a light up ahead, or rather two lights. It looks like signaling. I thought I could read semaphore, but—"

"Maybe I can read it," said Nelson eagerly. Either his eyes were a little sharper, or else he was more accustomed to Ted's signals, for in a minute he shouted: "It's Ted! He says Joey is safe in a cabin, and he wants us to come up."

Within minutes the news was flashed back to the Y camp via the mobile unit, and from there, they hoped, would quickly reach Joey's mother. Ted had signaled from the top of a hill, and it was decided that only Nelson, Woody, Ronald, Ken, and Mr. Krillman would make the rather difficult climb. The others remained at the tent, where refreshments were announced.

With their spirits vastly relieved, the climbers enjoyed themselves, as they fought their way to the summit. From the top they could see the cabin which had not been visible from below, and made their way to it.

They found Ted, Joey, and Argus all there, in good spirits and unharmed. Ted had built a roaring fire in the fireplace, and also lit a kerosene lamp he had found. They had also found some refreshments, and eaten a satisfactory snack, with the dog getting his share.

Ronald looked around. "It looks like somebody's been staying here, doesn't it?"

"There's been someone here, all right," Ted replied. "And this was the cabin where Argus stayed last night, because I found his collar still tied to a rope. He must have slipped out of his collar and then sneaked out the door, maybe when the man was bringing in wood."

"But what man?" Ken wanted to know. "Who is it that's been staying here, and what did he want? I've a notion it was someone who knows more about what was going on than any of us do."

"He knew more than we did about one thing, at least," Ted continued. "That's why I wanted you to come up here. Look over on the table."

He led the way to the side of the room, holding the lamp high. They grouped themselves closely about the table, studying what appeared to be some sort of document, carefully preserved between sheets of glass.

"Why, it looks like the missing treaty," Mr. Krillman exclaimed. "Now doesn't that beat everything?"

"I thought it would be all shriveled up by this time," Nelson remarked.

"Not necessarily," said the counselor. "Heat, air, and moisture are the chief enemies of old papers. But written on a good parchment and buried in an airtight metal box, it might last for a remarkably long time. Of course it must have required careful handling when it was removed from the box, and apparently this person took all proper pains."

"If this is the missing treaty, is it going to help the camp?" asked Ted.

"Definitely, not so much because it is the treaty, but because it will establish the proper boundary. I think we've got enough to go on now to identify the serpent rock for certain." He looked toward Woody. "If that should happen, there would no longer be any reason why lumbering shouldn't begin within a matter of weeks."

It was now Woody Preston's turn to look much happier.

"But what man?" Ken repeated. "That's what I'd like to know."

"I have a feeling," said Ronald speculatively, "that we've got the solution to the whole mystery right here in front of us. That is, I think each of us has different pieces to the solution, and that if we put them all together, we ought to be able to come up with the right answer."

Ronald looked at Ken. "Will you start off, Ken? Is there anything you want to tell us as your contribution to this conference?"

Ken shrugged. "I don't mind, now that our Thursday deadline is safely passed and you'll be reading it tomorrow in the *News-Record*. It isn't a great story, and doesn't go far toward solving the mystery, but it's something. Let me tell you it kept me scurrying around pretty swiftly this morning, trying to beat the deadline. Anyway, it's this: I can tell you what makes the trees sing.

"Actually the trees don't sing at all. The music seems to come from all around, and since the trees are all around, the listener naturally leaps to the conclusion that the music comes from the trees. Actually it comes from the rocks, although to me singing rocks are just as strange a phenomenon as singing trees. The rocks about here are of volcanic origin, and frequently porous in nature. It could easily happen that a great many of them have eroded through, or part way through, and they act as a sounding chamber when the wind blows through. I suppose, when the wind blows harder, it finds additional outlets, and this serves to change the pitch of the music, or to add chords to it. When the wind is blowing in changing gusts, the result could be something very much like a melody."

"Then it is the wind that's responsible," Mr. Krillman remarked. "That would probably explain why the singing is most common during the equinoctial storms of spring and fall. I suppose that wind direction is also important. It also helps explain why none of our hikers ever found the valley. It's very secluded, and probably the singing wouldn't be heard during the summer unless a thunderstorm were coming up, in which case the stray hiker would probably be more concerned about getting to shelter than in listening for the singing trees. I've heard of whistling rocks before, and I imagine this is the same thing, carried out to an unusual degree."

Ronald then took the floor. "Now I suppose it's my turn to make my contribution—Ted's and mine—to the general information pool. We would have liked the story for the *Town Crier*, but we've missed the deadline on that, and if there's to be police action within the next few days, the story will be public property by Monday's deadline. That means there won't be an exclusive for anyone.

"However that may be, Ted and I have come up with a possible motivation for the vandalism. Along the western side of the ravine Ted found some rock samples that aroused first his interest and then his suspicions. I had them analyzed by a geologist yesterday, and my results seemed so important that I took them around to the *Town Crier* office this morning. These rocks were actually copper ore, probably existing in commercial quantities, although the geologist couldn't be sure about that without visiting the location. So someone did have a good motive for driving the Y camp off the tract."

"How could that be?" asked Ted. "The mine is on Mr. Thompkins' property, isn't it?"

"Yes, or at least we all thought so, but remember the dispute over the boundary. No one was able to tell for sure exactly where the boundary is, at least until this treaty was found. We don't know for sure even now, although I imagine the man who was staying in this cabin knows. That must have been his purpose for being here."

"Then is that the reason for the fire?" Nelson inquired. "The man thought the mine was on Y property, so he planned to burn the camp out to make it move, and he could buy the tract?"

"Yes, I believe it was something like that," Ronald agreed.

"Then what about the vandalism?" asked Mr. Krillman.

"Well, he might have had several motives there. Perhaps he was simply angry at the camp and its directors for standing in the way of his plans. Possibly he thought that the damage would encourage the camp to sell all its trees and move away. But I think there may have been another reason. He was worried lest blame for the fire should fall on him, and he wanted to do something else that would seem to throw the blame on young vandals."

Mr. Krillman was thoughtful. "This, sounds convincing—all except for one thing. If the mine is where you say, I'm sure it isn't on Y property. The ravine was always accepted as the boundary."

"But it might have been a difficult matter to prove," Ronald pointed out. "As I remember that ravine, it branches off into several different heads, and with the water dried up, it would be difficult to say for certain which was the original course. With the land of little value for farming purposes, it would make very little difference, but with a mine there it could make all the difference in the world."

"And who is this man?" said Ken restlessly. "Is it somebody we know? I always had a hunch it was, because he seemed to know too much about what was going on."

Suddenly Nelson dived toward the bunk, under which a small object had caught his attention. He came up with it and held it aloft. It was a yellow-checked hunting cap.

"That hat!" Ted exclaimed in great surprise. "We've just seen one like that."

"Sure we did," Nelson agreed. "This is Mr. Thompkins' hat! He must be the man in the cabin."

They stared in silence at this strange clue which seemed to offer the last link in the mystery.

"But why did he do it," asked Nelson at last, "if the mine is on his own property?"

"Probably because he wasn't sure," Ronald suggested, "or he may have thought the vein extended over on to Y property, and he wanted it all for himself."

Mr. Krillman said slowly, "I've had some dealings with Mr. Thompkins before. He's a highly suspicious man. He may have been afraid to try to reach a boundary agreement with us, because he feared we would try to get his mine away from him. If the camp had burned down and we were forced to move away, we would have had to make sure about the boundary before we sold the land. Maybe that was what he was trying to get us to do—agree to the ravine as a boundary, all without knowing about his mine."

"That digging around the serpent rock looked rather recent," Nelson recollected. "It must have been only a little while ago that he found the treaty."

"Yes," Ronald continued, "and because it now proved his right to the mine, he left it out here where we could find it. Otherwise, I feel sure he would have destroyed it."

"But why did he use this cabin?" asked Ted. "He could have worked from his farm."

"This made a convenient base from which to carry on his search for the treaty," Ken pointed out. "Besides, maybe he didn't want his wife or his neighbors to guess what he was up to."

"Maybe so," Ronald laughed, "but I suspect he's a little deeper man than you think. Look how he left all the evidence around to show that someone had been living here. Remember that he didn't mind showing himself to Joey, although he must have known Joey would tell us about him. And he wore orange sunglasses as a sort of disguise. I believe he was trying to create a mythical man for us. If we tried to pin the vandalism on him, he could say, 'What are you bothering me about? The man you want is the one who stayed up in the cabin.' And he might have gotten away with it, if he hadn't lost his hat."

"The day he found Joey," Ted recalled, "he must have gone home immediately afterward, thinking we might try to find the cabin Joey would tell us about. He must have just about reached his farm when Nelson and I saw him at the ravine."

Ronald turned to Mr. Krillman. "What do you think about it?"

"It sounds pretty logical to me," said the counselor grimly. "I believe the police will at least be interested in questioning Mr. Thompkins to see what he has to say."

"Well, that's our case," Ken summarized. "I must say this business has led me off on so many wrong tangents, mostly bed mattresses filled with Confederate money, that I'm glad I can simmer down for a while... Say, isn't that coffee hot yet? Let's have a cup, and get out of this dismal place."

CHAPTER 21

Better Luck Next Time

Mr. Thompkins was easily picked up by the police, but at first denied everything. As Ted had foretold, it turned out that he had a number of scratches on his arms which he could not explain, and starting from there the police were partially able to break down his story.

There seemed little doubt that his motive for the fire was to force the camp to move, and either sell the land to him or at least reach a boundary agreement. If the camp had moved, or even if it was decided to rebuild or reconstruct in the same place, the directors would have wanted to make sure about the boundary. Mr. Thompkins wanted the boundary settled, too, but he wanted the initiative to come from the Y. Ronald had summarized the reasons for the vandalism correctly, and Mr. Thompkins had hoped to blame young offenders for everything. Nor did he ever show much contrition over this. "It's just the sort of thing those young hoodlums would do, anyway," he explained.

There was a high degree of stupidity about the whole affair. The mine was on Mr. Thompkins own property, and he might have developed it as he saw fit. But being suspicious of the camp's directors, and annoyed by the nearby presence of the camp anyway, he had tried first to destroy the camp by fire, and then to damage it severely by vandalism. As it had appeared from the very first, there was a certain element of irrationality about the entire thing.

The possible prosecution of Mr. Thompkins proved a difficult matter. Although he had admitted most of these things, he refused to sign a confession, and if he chose to deny them later in court, it might have been very difficult to prove the case against him. When he agreed to pay for all the damage he had caused, Mr. Blair decided in view of everything to accept the offer, provided Mr. Thompkins also sell his farm and copper mine for a fair price and move away.

Why he had not smashed the Trailside Museum was never explained, so each person had his own theory about it. Nelson thought he had merely missed it in the dark, as they had first supposed. Ted thought that since

Mr. Thompkins was trying to make this look like the work of juvenile delinquents, he may have hesitated to smash the museum, feeling that teenagers might also have hesitated, not being certain of the value of the exhibits. It was Ken who perhaps made the shrewdest observation of all.

"I think he wasn't sure how valuable the exhibits might be, and in case he was discovered and wanted to buy his way out—as eventually happened—he didn't want to be in over his head financially."

At the end of the week, the campers prepared to break camp and return home. Before going the boys had a parting word for Woody Preston.

"Now that you're coming back to school," Ted invited, "if you're interested in newspaper work come around to the office. We can always use more reporters."

"Sure," Nelson added, "and the track team's starting indoor practice, so if you feel like trying out for something, come on down to the gym and I'll introduce you around. Those long legs of yours ought to be good for something."

"Thanks, I will," said Woody gratefully.

Afterward Ted remarked to Nelson, "I hope this eye of mine looks better by Monday."

"It won't," Nelson assured him. "Let's face it, you're going to have about fifteen thousand people asking you what happened to it."

"I don't mind that. I don't mind anything right now. I'm feeling so much better about a certain editorial that's coming out in the school paper next week that I don't care what anybody says about anything else."

"Well, Ted," Ronald told him, "you turned out to be right this time, but don't let it swell your hatband. Just being right once doesn't turn all teenagers into angels."

"No," Ted agreed happily. "I'm just glad I was right this once."

Most of the snow, a smaller fall than predicted, had melted under the warm spring sun, except where it had drifted up, and the piles lay dirty and forlorn, with a little trickle of water leading away from each. The ground was soggy beneath their feet as they walked to the cars. Ted, Nelson and Ronald were to ride in Ken's car.

"What is there about you three," Nelson deliberated, "that makes you different from other people? I used to lead such a peaceful existence before I took up with Ted, and now I seem to be up to my ears in trouble all the time."

"Maybe," Ted explained, "being associated with a newspaper, you get leads on all the big things that are going on. Or maybe a newspaperman needs the type of nose that just naturally shoves itself into everybody's business. Anyway, it makes life interesting."

"Let's try to figure up what we got out of this business," Ken remarked. "Ted feels better about his editorial. There wasn't much of a story about the vandalism for the Town *Crier*, since they couldn't verify the rock samples in time, but their story on the trailerites went over big, so they can't complain. Anything for you, Ron?"

"Well, the vandalism was too far away to interest big-city readers, but that yarn about the Indians and the singing trees might make a Sunday feature-section story. I may try my hand at it."

"Some vacation for you," Ted interjected.

"And I picked up three little stories," Ken concluded. "I cleared Mr. and Mrs. Parsons of stealing Mr. Raeburn's money, I explained the singing trees, and I'll have a report on the police questioning of Mr. Thompkins, which will probably be somewhat inconclusive, and in any case won't be an exclusive for my paper. I picked up some minnows, but as usual the big fish got away."

Ted was satisfied with the way things turned out, and Ronald, although he sympathized with Ken, remembered all too well the times his rival had beat him out in the past.

"Oh, well," he consoled his friend, "better luck next time."

www.ingramcontent.com/pod-product-compliance
Lightning Source LLC
Chambersburg PA
CBHW050802250626
47155CB00005B/2174